Dr. Elena Gladstone was an experimenter. And even after hundreds of experiments, she never lost her sense of wonder that a learned response, such as fear trained into an animal, would produce a substance in the animal's brain that could be isolated, purified, and intensified so that it could be injected into the bloodstream of another animal . . . and produce exactly the same fear.

She never published any of her research. Somehow, in the back of her mind, there had always been a feeling that there was a profit to be turned through this research. This profit, she figured, would be in direct proportion to how much she knew and how little others knew.

Might this not be a terrific way for our fearless hero, Remo, to finally get a taste of fear?

THE DESTROYER SERIES:

ATTENTION: SCHOOLS AND CORPORATIONS

PINNACLE Books are available at quantity discounts with bulk purchases for educational, business or special promotional use. For further details, please write to: SPECIAL SALES MANAGER, Pinnacle Books, Inc. 1430 Broadway, New York, NY 10018.

WRITE FOR OUR FREE CATALOG

If there is a Pinnacle Book you want—and you cannot find it locally—it is available from us simply by sending the title and price plus 75¢ to cover mailing and handling costs to:

Pinnacle Books, Inc.
Reader Service Department
1430 Broadway
New York, NY 10018

Please allow 6 weeks for delivery.

—— Check here if you want to receive our catalog regularly.

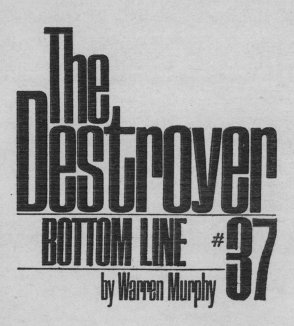

The Destroyer

BOTTOM LINE #37

by Warren Murphy

PINNACLE BOOKS • NEW YORK

This is a work of fiction. All the characters and events portrayed in this book are fictional, and any resemblance to real people or incidents is purely coincidental.

DESTROYER #37: BOTTOM LINE

Copyright © 1979 by Richard Sapir and Warren Murphy

All rights reserved, including the right to reproduce this book or portions thereof in any form.

An original Pinnacle Books edition, published for the first time anywhere.

First printing, July 1979
Second printing, May 1980
Third printing, February 1981

ISBN: 0-523-41252-5

Cover illustration by Hector Garrido

Printed in the United States of America

PINNACLE BOOKS, INC.
1430 Broadway
New York, New York 10018

CHAPTER ONE

If distrusting people had been an Olympic event, Zack Meadows would have scored perfect tens.

He did not trust jockeys with Italian names. He was convinced they sat around in the clubhouse, hours before the races, deciding who was going to win what. How they always managed to select winning horses on which Zack Meadows didn't have a bet, he ascribed to simple Mediterranean deviousness.

He didn't trust policemen. He had never met a cop who wasn't on the take and who didn't have a summer house. Nor did he trust civil service examiners. Because three times they had turned him down for appointment to the police department, a job he wanted badly so he could go on the take and buy a summer house. He also didn't trust real estate people who sold summer houses.

Zack Meadows did not trust women who came to him and said they wanted their husband followed because he was running around with another woman. This usually meant the wife was hooked on another man at the moment and was thinking of divorce but would probably soon change her mind and try to beat Meadows out of his fee. Meadows handled this

1

by first following the wife who hired him to find out who she was running around with, then if she dropped him later, he would peddle the information to the husband.

Nor did he trust swarthy people, guys who sold hot watches, blacks, liberals, cab drivers, Jews, doctors, bookies, life insurance companies, American car manufacturers, foreign car manufacturers, and places that claimed they could replace your car's muffler in twenty minutes for $14.95.

Not that he regarded himself as distrusting. He thought he was softhearted, the original patsy, just occasionally working his way toward realism. Being suspicious was just part of an urban survival kit in dog-eat-dog New York City. Zack Meadows sometimes thought he might be happier living in the north woods in a log cabin. But he didn't trust well water and who in his right mind would trust animals not to attack when your back was turned?

So why did he trust this nervous little man who sat in front of Meadows's cigarette-scarred desk, twisting his gloves nervously in his hands, and having difficulty meeting Meadows's bleary-eyed gaze? Particularly when the man's story made no sense; he had trouble telling it, and after ten minutes he still hadn't been able to get it out.

"Now let's try again," Meadows said. "You're starting to eat up a lot of time and I'm not making any money sitting here listening to you yap."

The little man sighed. He was delicate appearing with long thin hands and the skin of his fingers bore brown blotches as if he made his living working with chemicals.

2

"Have you ever heard of the Lippincott family?" he asked.

"No," said Meadows. "The last car I owned was built by one of their companies and I bought gas from their oil companies and I'm in hock to six of their banks and if I ever get any time off I watch television on networks that they own. The only thing I don't have is pictures of them on my money and I figure that'll be next when they buy the rest of the country. Of course, I heard of the Lippincott family, you think I'm stupid?" Meadows took a deep breath that raised his shoulders and expanded his fatty cheeks. Sitting behind his desk, he looked like an outraged blowfish.

The small man seemed to tremble. He raised a hand as if to ward off an attack.

"No, no, I didn't mean that," he said quickly. "That's just a way of speaking."

"Yeah," growled Meadows. He wondered if this guy would be done before it was time for him to call his bookie. There were Italian jockeys riding in both the first and second today at Belmont. It was a sure daily double.

"Well, the Lippincotts," the man said nervously. He glanced toward the door of the seedy third-floor office and then leaned closer to Meadows. "Somebody is trying to kill them."

Meadows sat back in his squeaking swivel chair and folded his arms. He assumed his expression of disgust. "Sure," he said. "Who? England? France? One of them nigger countries that change their name every week? Who the hell can kill the Lippincotts without declaring war on America first?"

3

"But someone is," the little man said. His eyes met Meadows directly. Meadows looked away.

"So what are you telling me for?" he asked. "What's it to me or you or anybody?"

"Because the Lippincotts don't know about it but I know. I know who's going to try to kill them."

"And?"

"I think saving their lives ought to be worth a lot of money to us."

"Why us?" asked Meadows.

"Because I can't do it myself," the little man said. Sentence by sentence, his voice was getting stronger. His hands were no longer wringing out his gloves. It was as if, once having taken the first step, he was committed and with the commitment came an end to nervousness about what he was doing.

His name was Jasper Stevens. He was a medical technician and he worked for a private research laboratory that was funded by the Lippincott Foundation. As he talked, Meadows tried to picture the Lippincott family in his mind.

There was the father, Elmer Lippincott. He was eighty years old but nobody had told him, so he acted like thirty. He had just married some young blonde. He had made his fortune starting as a roustabout in the oil fields and as he admitted in later life, "I got rich because I was a bigger bastard then anybody else there." He had the face and eyes of a hawk. The press sometimes referred to him as an eccentric but that wasn't really true. It was just that the elder Lippincott, dubbed "The First," did just what he damn well pleased.

He had three sons. Elmer Jr. was called "Lem," and he was a kind of superboss who handled all the

4

Lippincott manufacturing interests: car companies, television factories, modular home construction.

Randall was the second son, in charge of the family's finances. He ran the banks, the mutual funds, the brokerage houses, and the overseas investment companies.

Douglas, the youngest son, was the diplomat. He testified before the government when they were discussing tax incentives and balance of payments and how to improve trade. He dealt with the heads of foreign countries when the Lippincotts wanted to start some new oil exploration or build a new overseas auto plant.

Meadows was surprised at how much he remembered about them. He had seen an article about them in one of those people magazines a month earlier when he had gotten a haircut. It was an old magazine, without a cover, on the barber's table. Inside there was a picture of the Lippincott family.

There was Elmer the First, seated in the back, with his new blonde young wife standing by his side. And standing on the other side of the chair were the three Lippincott sons. Meadows had been surprised at how little they looked like their father. There was no steel in their faces, no hardness. They had the look of soft, well-fed men, and he remembered having thought that it was a good thing that the old man had been the oil roustabout and not his sons because they didn't look like they could fight their way in out of the rain. Except for maybe the youngest one, Douglas. At least he had a chin.

It took two hours for Jasper Stevens to tell his story to Zack Meadows because it had a lot of technical terms in it and Meadows kept going back over it and over it, trying to get it clear in his mind, but also trying to trip Stevens up in an untruth. But the man's story was consistent. Meadows found himself believing him.

Finally, Meadows said "So why'd you come to me?"

Jasper Stevens smiled. "I think somebody should be willing to pay handsomely for all the information I've got. And I don't know how to go about it."

Meadows laughed and Stevens winced. "Information? You don't have anything. You've got a few facts and a couple of names and some ideas. But you don't have any evidence. Nothing written down. No reports. Nothing that couldn't be denied by somebody just saying that you're a liar."

Stevens began twisting his gloves again.

"But you believe me, don't you?" He made it seem very important to him.

Meadows thought for a moment. "Yeah, I believe you. I don't know why but I do."

This turned out to be critical because Jasper Stevens had no money with which to pay Zack Meadows for his time, but the deal they quickly arranged was a fifty-fifty split of anything they got from the Lippincott family. Stevens nodded glumly. He had apparently been expecting a bigger share.

After Stevens had gone, Meadows sat for a long time in his chair, trying to avoid the lumpy tape patches that covered the rips in the chair, which he had found in the street one night several blocks from his ratty office on Twenty-sixth Street. Then he got tired of all that thinking and decided to save himself the bookie's vigorish and went to Belmont where the

Italian-surnamed jockeys in the first and second races ran dead last.

Flossie was lying on her bed, eating chocolates and watching television, when Meadows let himself into her apartment, using an entire ring of keys to get past her battery of anti-burglar locks and bars and alarms.

He and Flossie had been "going together" for five years. Meadows spent most nights at her apartment and even though she was the one person in the world he totally trusted, she did not have a key to his apartment farther downtown. Nor had he any plans to give her one.

She looked up as he finally got past the last burglar barrier. She was wearing a pink negligee that was frayed at the edges. On her ample belly were chips of chocolate from the family-sized bar of Nestle's Crunch she was eating. Her dyed blonde hair was uncombed.

"If it isn't the world's greatest gumshoe," she said.

Meadows carefully relocked all the security devices before turning around and announcing, "I've got a big case."

Flossie looked interested. "Oh? How much retainer?"

"None yet," Meadows said.

She looked away from him in disgust and turned back to her black and white television set where four people, obviously chosen for serious genetic defects, were attempting to win a dollar and change by making fools of themselves, something God had already seen to at the moment of their births.

"Yeah," she sneered. "Real big case."

"It is," he said. "It really is."

"I'll believe it when I see some green."

7

"Green, hah? Well, let me ask you this, lady. You ever hear of the Lippincott family?"

"Of course I heard of the Lippincott family. You think I'm stupid?"

"Well . . ."

"They hired *you*?" Flossie asked. She adopted a pose of full attention as if ready to make the great effort to rise from the bed if the answer was what she wanted to hear.

"Not exactly."

Flossie collapsed back onto her three pillows, like a punctured balloon.

"But I'm going to save their lives," Meadows said.

Rising almost up once had been enough for Flossie, particularly when it turned out to be a false alarm. She contented herself with "Yeah, sure. And Idi Amin wants me to marry him."

"Not likely," said Meadows. "He likes his women skinny."

"Oh, yeah," said Flossie. She choked on a rice krispie imbedded in the chocolate and coughed a lot. When her breath returned, she said, "Oh, yeah? Well, you want yourself a skinny blonde, you go get one. See if they put up with you for long, big gumshoe."

Suddenly it became very important to Zack Meadows that he impress Flossie. He went to the kitchen table, swept aside the debris with his arm, and picked up a yellow pad and a ballpoint pen that commemorated the opening of a new ribs joint on Twenty-third Street.

"What are you doing?" Flossie demanded.

"Important case. Got to put it all down."

"Oh, yeah. The Lippincott case," she said.

"It really is," said Meadows. He wondered why he went to such lengths to please Flossie, who had been a stripper till she got old and a prostitute till she got fat, and then was just a barfly hanging around the West Side bars, cadging drinks, when Meadows met her. She held the space in his heart that some men filled by owning a dog. Meadows didn't trust dogs; they seemed always to be conniving, preparing to bite him. And if Flossie's disposition wasn't exactly the unquestioning devotion of a Great Dane, it wasn't bad either. Meadows had always mistrusted women, but somehow he felt sure that Flossie wasn't about to go tipping on him.

And besides, her dirty little apartment was only two blocks from his office and it was a good place to flop when he didn't want to ride the subway home.

He worked on his notes for two hours, trying to write out the story Jasper Stevens had told him. The floor near the table was covered with crumpled yellow sheets that Meadows threw away because they didn't have just the touch he wanted.

"What's that?" Flossie asked. "A fan letter to Elmer Lippincott?"

"Business," Meadows said.

"Yeah, sure," Flossie said. Meadows heard her flicking channels on the TV set, looking for the most insipid of the game shows, turning up the volume to annoy him. He smiled to himself; she wanted him to pay attention to her, that was all.

But he had other things to do.

When he was finally done with the letter, which turned out to be half the size he expected it to be, he stood up and looked over at her with a triumphant smile.

9

"You got an envelope around here?"

"Try the drawer under the sink. There's Christmas cards and things in there," she said.

Meadows rooted around in the drawer until he came up with a blue-tinted envelope almost six inches square and he folded his yellow pages neatly and stuffed them into the envelope. It already had a stamp on it. Meadows knew Flossie was watching as he sealed the envelope and printed an address on it.

He walked to her side and casually dropped the envelope onto her big belly.

"If anything happens to me, I want you to promise that you'll see that gets delivered."

Flossie glanced down. The envelope was addressed to: "The President of the U.S., Washington, Personal and Confidential."

He expected her to be impressed. She looked at him and said "What's going to happen to *you*?"

"You never know," he said. He turned toward the door.

"Hey, you're serious, aren't you?" Flossie said.

He nodded without turning.

"You going to take care of yourself?"

"You know it," he said.

"I wouldn't want anything to happen to you."

"I know," Meadows said.

"Before you leave, would you get me the bottle of Fleischmann's under the sink?"

He handed her the bottle, let himself out through all the burglar barriers, and started downstairs. Inside the apartment, Flossie took a swig from the bottle of rye, looked at the envelope, smirked and tossed it toward the corner. It landed on a pile of clothes.

Meadows allowed himself the unaccustomed luxury of a taxicab to get to the Lifeline Laboratory. It was in a brownstone building on East Eighty-first Street, a building distinguished from its neighbors only by the visible fact that it had a small identifying plaque next to the front door, and the invisible fact that it alone, of all the buildings on the block, was not overrun with roaches, a condition New Yorkers accepted with their accustomed stolidity despite the fact that apartments on the street rented for $275 a room.

There was only a small light in the front window of the Lifeline Laboratory, and Meadows walked quietly around the back. There was no sign of a burglar alarm on the back door. This probably meant one of three things: one, there was a hidden burglar alarm. This was highly unlikely because the primary use of a burglar alarm in New York City—where the police could take thirty minutes to respond to a call, thus allowing burglars to strip everything including the wallpaper from the walls—was as a deterrent. Therefore, the more visible the alarm the better.

Two, there might be a guard on duty. Meadows decided to hold that in abeyance.

Three, the people at Lifeline Laboratory were nuts and didn't think they'd be burglarized.

Meadows decided that nobody was that crazy so he rejected that possibility. Back to possibility two: the laboratory had a guard on duty. That was probably the light in the front of the building.

Zack Meadows didn't trust guards. He had been a private guard once and knew what they did. They brought their bottle, their girlie magazines, and thirty

11

minutes after everybody went home for the night, they fell asleep.

He got into the building by slipping the back lock with an expired credit card. Meadows didn't carry credit cards anymore because he could never remember what he had charged and he was sure the credit card company was making up most of the items on his statement.

Enough light came through the uncovered windows for him to be able to walk through the dark laboratory. It was a large room with tall laboratory tables, eight feet long, topped with white formica. There were five of them in a row on his right side. On his left were cages, stacked neatly from floor to ceiling, and he was startled for a moment when he heard the high-pitched squeaking of rats, but then he realized they were safe in the cages. There were other animals in cages too, but he could not tell what they were in the semi-darkness and he was careful not to walk too close to them.

He walked toward the front of the building. Through the window in the door on the far end of the room, he peered down a long hallway toward a front reception room. Meadows could see a pair of feet propped up on a desk. Men's shoes, blue trousers. A desk drawer was open and a bottle of scotch was protruding from it.

He nodded to himself, pulled down the shade on the inside of the laboratory door, then pulled the shades on all the windows and the back door before flicking on a light. He locked the door leading to the rest of the building. If he heard the guard stirring, he could turn off the light and flee the building before the man could get into the room.

12

The place was like a zoo, he thought. The entire side wall was covered with cages and inside the cages were rats and monkeys and some kind of lizards and even bowls of worms.

Jasper Stevens had told him about the animals but he had wanted to see for himself.

There was one small cage whose glass was painted black. Attached to the front of the cage was an eyepiece so an observer could press his face to it and look inside the cage.

Zack Meadows pressed his face to the eyepiece. A pair of rats ran around inside the big fishtank. An overhead light brilliantly illuminated the cage. If what Jasper said was true. . . .

Meadows turned off the overhead light inside the cage. Enough light drifted in through the sides for Meadows to see in through the eyepiece. As soon as the light went off, the two rats scurried into a corner and huddled there, squeaking and shivering, the terror that racked their bodies total and crushing.

Rats afraid of the dark? Jasper Stevens had told him that but he hadn't really believed it.

"Yes, that's right, Mr. Meadows. They're afraid of the dark," said a voice behind him.

Meadows wheeled and blinked his eyes once as the strong overhead fluorescent lighting contracted his pupils.

Standing just inside the connecting door was the most beautiful woman he had ever seen. She had flaming red hair and a complexion that made him understand what people meant when they said creamy skin. She was wearing a light tan sweater with a brown suede skirt and a matching leather vest. She was smiling at him and if a woman who looked like that had smiled at him on the street, it would have made his day. His week. His month.

But this smile didn't seem all that warm and cozying, because the woman held a .38 revolver in her right hand, pointing unwaveringly at him. She looked as if she had held that gun before and knew what to do with it.

"How'd you know my name?" he asked.

The woman ignored the question. "We have other rats who are afraid of other things," she said. "And other animals too. Not just rats. It's amazing, with a little electric shock, a little starvation, a little heat applied to the genitals, you can teach any animal to be afraid of anything."

Meadows found himself nodding. Jasper Stevens had explained all this to him in the afternoon. He wished that he had been able to understand more of it. There was something about animals, when they learned to be afraid of something, they created some kind of proteins in their brains. And then if you injected those proteins into other animals, they would instantly become afraid of what the first animals were afraid of. It had sounded like bullshit to Zack Meadows. It still did.

"How'd you know my name?" he repeated.

"And just what is it you're afraid of, Mr. Meadows?" the woman asked him. She still had that smile on her full lips, her mouth shining brightly. It looked as if she had just licked her lips with wet tongue.

"Nothing, lady," said Meadows. "I'm not afraid of you and not that gun either." He waved a hand at her, and turned to walk toward the back door. His senses were sharp, waiting to hear the cock of the revolver's hammer.

14

There was no sound.

Just as he extended his hand toward the doorknob, the back door pulled open. There were two men standing there, wearing white laboratory clothes. Big men.

Before he could run, they had his arms pinned between them, and turned him around to the woman.

She returned the pistol to the purse she had placed on the lab table. Meadows noticed that it was also brown suede. He liked women who coordinated their clothes. He doubted if telling her that would make much difference.

"So you're not afraid of anything?" she said. "We'll just have to see about that, Mr. Meadows."

"I asked you. How do you know my name?"

"I'm afraid your friend, Jasper Stevens, was careless."

Meadows shook his head. "I hate careless people," he said.

The woman nodded. "That's right. Carelessness kills."

The two men hustled Meadows down a short corridor to a small office off the laboratory. There were two tall filing cabinets in the corner, and when one of the men pressed a button on the bookshelf, the filing cabinets swung away from the wall, exposing a flight of stairs leading down to a basement. Behind him, Meadows heard the redhead calling out to the guard.

"Everything's all right, Herman."

"That's good, Dr. Gladstone," he said.

His voice didn't sound like that of a drunk, Meadows thought. Suddenly he thought of a fourth reason why he might not have seen a burglar alarm. The alarm had been hidden. A trap had been set and he had fallen into it.

Downstairs, he was pushed into a room with two metal cots in it. On one of the cots was Jasper Stevens. He was curled up in a fetal postion and his eyes opened wide with shock when the door opened.

"You jerkoff," Meadows growled. "This is what I get for being so trusting."

He was ticked and he was still ticked when they locked the door and even more ticked a half hour later when the two men came back and held him down and the redheaded Dr. Gladstone injected something into his neck and then into Jasper's, and then unconsciousness overtook him.

He didn't know how long he was unconscious, but when he woke his hands and feet were tied and he was blindfolded. His fingertips hurt and when he touched his thumb to his fingers, he felt them raw and mushy under his touch.

But that did not bother him. It was something else. He heard the roar of an engine and the slapping of water against the sides of a boat, and even though he had gone through four years of the Navy without ever getting seasick, this was something else and he felt the bile rising in his throat and he fought back the impulse to throw up because with the gag in his mouth he would likely choke on his own vomit.

Water. A watery grave. He felt sweat break out all over his body and then turn to a cold chill. He was a strong swimmer or had been before bourbon had turned muscle to fat but he knew now that he could not survive for a moment in water. The thought of it filled him with dread. Water surrounding his body.

16

Blocking his nose. Making it impossible to breathe. His body struggling, gasping, trying to get breath, and when he opened his mouth, even more of the water pouring in, trying to fight its way down into his lungs, to blow them up like big balloons and then to burst them and spill his guts and his life all over the sea where fishes could feed on him.

He fainted.

When he woke again, there was still the sound of a boat engine and still the sound of water, but he wondered why he felt no sense of movement if he was on a boat.

He heard Dr. Gladstone's voice. "Still not afraid of anything, Mr. Meadows?" she asked mockingly. "You realize where you are? At sea. That's water all around you. Water. Cold, dark water."

Meadows tried to scream but the gag muffled all sound. Then the blindfold was removed and the gag was pulled from his mouth. He wasn't in water. He was standing near the edge of some kind of lake. Dr. Gladstone was in front of him and the two big men were standing behind him. Jasper Stevens was still unconscious on the ground.

"Help me. I'll do anything," Meadows pleaded. "Help me."

"Sorry, friend," she said coldly. "Enjoy your bath."

Meadows felt the ropes being removed from his arms and legs and then he was lifted up into the air by the two men, swung back and forth and then tossed out into the lake. A moment later, Jasper Stevens followed.

Meadows hit with a splash. He could feel the water wet his clothes and he screamed. He was surrounded by water. It was all around him. He tried to climb on top of Jasper Stevens to get away from the water, but Jasper fought him off and tried to climb on top of Meadows. Meadows felt the water all over him and the fear of it brought tears to his eyes and he could feel his heart racing in panic, and then as the water reached his neck, he could feel his heart stopping, but before his brain stopped too, he saw Jasper Stevens in front of him, floating, and the small man's eyes already had glazed over and Meadows knew he was dead and knew he himself would be dead in a moment and he welcomed death because anything was better than the water.

And so he died, and his body and that of Jasper Stevens floated among the orange peels and pop bottles on top of 17 inches of water in the lake in Central Park.

Dr. Gladstone picked up the tiny cassette tape recorder with the boat and water sounds on it, turned it off and put it into her pocket. She smiled at her two attendants and they left Central Park to go back to the Lifeline Laboratory.

The bodies of Zack Meadows and Jasper Stevens were pulled from the lake the next morning by police who had been called to the scene by the 262nd jogger to pass the lake and notice the two floating bodies. The first 261 hadn't wanted to get involved.

The medical examiner said both men had died of heart attacks. No one thought it strange that both men's fingertips had been mutilated to prevent fingerprint identification, or that two men should choose the Central Park lake in which to have simultaneous heart attacks. The commander of the Central

Park police precinct was happy when the heart attack report came back, because if the two floaters had been murdered, he would have had to put some men on duty investigating the murders, and all his men were now busy patrolling the park, giving tickets to people who failed to clean up after their dogs, and watching for other such serious crimes.

So with no identification and no investigation, no one ever thought to question Flossie, who lay in her bed, eating chocolates, drinking Fleischmann straight, and watching game shows.

When Zack Meadows did not come back to her for three days, she decided he was gone. She didn't think he was dead. Enough men had left her in her life for her to know that it didn't take death to bring it about.

On the fourth day, her last bottle of Fleischmann's was gone, so she got out of bed and dusted herself with a dry washcloth. She combed the front of her hair and put on lipstick. She looked around for a dress and found several in a pile of clothes in the corner of the room. She took the one that looked least dirty.

It was a red and blue flowered print that made her look like a sofa. But the neckline was cut low and her giant bosom and cleavage were visible, and since she had to find someone to buy her a bottle, the dress would do. Tit men, she had realized early in life, were not terribly particular. Big was beautiful to them.

As she picked up the dress, a light blue envelope fluttered to the floor. She picked it up and looked at it. She had never seen it before. It was addressed to the President of the United States and had a stamp on it.

She wondered if she could get the stamp off and sell it to somebody. She tried a corner but the stamp was firmly glued down.

Anyway, the letter was addressed to the President. It might be important.

She couldn't imagine how it had gotten into her apartment.

She held it in her hand as she slid the blue and red dress over her head and she was still squeezing the letter tightly in her hand as she walked ponderously down the three flights of stairs to the street. As she headed for the corner, she saw the red, white, and blue mailbox and it seemed appropriately colored to receive a letter for the President. She thought for a moment that perhaps the letter was some great spy secret and she maybe would get a medal and maybe a cash reward from the President, so she mailed the letter quickly, before realizing that her name and address weren't on it and they would have no way to track her down to give her her medal and her money.

The hell with medals and money. She wanted a drink. As she walked away, she decided that even if the President did send her a check, the post office would probably steal it. She didn't trust the post office. Somebody, a long time ago, had told her not to.

CHAPTER TWO

His name was Remo and he did not know fear. He knew the cold of the slick ice against his body in the dark mountains of New Hampshire. He knew the winds that could pop a person like a wicker ball down the midnight ravine, banging bones to pitiful chips in a skin-slit shell of organs that would no longer breathe or digest food or purify blood or pump that blood. He knew the winds. He knew force.

And because he understood it, not as some hostile deadly force, but as part of the same universe his breathing was part of, Remo Williams did not skid down the rock hard ice of the White Mountains in late December.

His body, lightly covered with black mesh, moved as if it had grown on this mountain, up with each reach and press, a perfect unity that needed no stairs or ladders or ropes, the things that other bodies, softer and unused bodies, required to move up a sheer ice cliff.

He moved now up the cliff, not even thinking of his breathing. He moved because he willed it and the many years of pain and wisdom that had brought him here with the winter taste in his mouth and the low moan of the spruce down below, made him a part of this universe that frightened so many men, which made others stiff of joints and, even worse, robbed them of their rhythms and of the timing that gave some men power.

Those other men had learned the wrong ways because their food was mush and their lives starved for the daily spring of survival. They had not learned that fear was like a mild hunger or a light chill. They had become unused to fear, so that from them it stole strength.

To this man with the thick wrists and thin body moving up into darkness under a black, cold sky, fear was, like his breathing, something else, something that existed apart from him, and because he did not need it to climb this slick curtain of glare ice, he did not call on it.

He came up over the top of the cliff with a small rolling motion that barely dented the deep fresh snow and then was standing at the top, looking at the brightly-lighted cabin, half-hidden behind a band of pine trees fifty yards away. He moved toward the cabin. His feet made no sound in the deep fresh snow. No puff of breath noisily escaped his lips, and he thought of the days when he clumped noisily down a flight of steps and puffed like a tea kettle climbing the same steps.

That had been years ago, but it had been more than years too. It had happened in a different lifetime.

He had been Remo Williams then, Patrolman Remo Williams in the Newark, New Jersey, police department, and he had been framed for a murder he hadn't committed and sentenced to an electric chair

22

that hadn't worked, and then resurrected to serve as the killer arm for a secret organization that fought crime in the United States.

That was what the organization, CURE, had contracted for, but what they got was something else. No one had known that the years of training and the discipline of body and mind would have changed Remo Williams from what he once was to . . . to what?

To what? Remo Williams grinned as he moved through the night. Not even he knew what he was. An ancient and wise Oriental sitting in a houseboat on the shore of Lake Winnepesaukee fifty miles away thought that Remo Williams was the reincarnation of Shiva, the Indian god of destruction. But the same wise Oriental thought that Barbra Streisand was America's most beautiful woman, that soap operas, before they got dirty and obscene, were America's only real art form, and that a depressing little fishing village in North Korea was the center of the universe.

So much for Shiva. Remo was not the reincarnation of a god, but he wasn't just a man either. He had become more. He had become what men could be, if they learned to use their bodies and their minds to the full extent of their powers.

"I'm a man," he said softly to himself, his whisper lost in the wail of wind through the trees. "That's got to be worth something."

Then he was standing alongside one of the windows of the cabin, listening to the voices inside.

There were four of them, four men talking. They were talking with the fearlessness of men who know that no one could reach them because the only way up to the cabin was along a twisting road, and that road was spotted with detection devices, and, for the last seventy-five yards to the cabin, with buried land mines.

So the members of the Cypriot Liberation Alliance felt quite free to discuss which kind of babies were best to plant dynamite sticks under. Little black babies or little blonde babies.

"Nobody touch a baby carriage, especially when you wheel it into a maternity ward," said one aloud.

"What that got to do with mainland Greeks?" asked another.

"We show them, Tilhas," said the first, "what we think of how they not help us when we attack the Turks and lose. All we have are the Palestinians, our spiritual brothers."

A third voice spoke up. "Anyone who can see the moral imperative in dynamiting babies as part of revolutionary justice knows and understands Greek Cypriot values," he said.

A fourth voice spoke. "We are victims. Imperialists are the oppressors."

The man called Tilhas who did not seem to understand all this blood lust asked "But why assault Americans?"

"Because they supply the Turks."

"But they supply us also."

"How can you call yourself a Cypriot if you don't blame others for what happens to you? If you put up a bad roof, blame corporate imperialism. If your daughter gets pregnant, blame Hollywood movies. When you rob your father and he breaks your bones for it, blame the Egyptians. You must remember at all times you are a Cypriot and that means you will never invent anything or build anything or grow anything anyone else will want. Therefore you can never be on the side of doers. They must always be your enemies, Tilhas. America is made up of the worst doers in the world. Therefore, we must hate them most. Besides, it's easiest to dynamite baby carriages here. If we get caught, nobody pulls our arms out our shoulders. Nobody peels our skin off our back. Nobody starts bonfires on our bare stomach. No one hurts us. They just put us in jail and let us go a little later."

"Wrong," came Remo's voice. He stood inside the door, looking around at the four men. "There are still some of us who think that evil ought to be punished."

"Who are you?" asked one of the Cypriots.

Remo raised a hand for silence. "Which one of you is Tilhas?"

A small man with a scraggly mustache and basset-hound eyes raised his hand meekly. "I Tilhas. Why?"

"I heard you from the window," Remo said. "I'm going to do you a favor. You're going to die easily."

He did. The others didn't.

Remo looked down at the thrashing body of the last one still to live.

"They'll find you in the spring," he said. "When they see what happened to you, I think everybody else in your ragtag little gang is going to go back to Cyprus and forget about dynamiting babies. So don't look at it like you're just dying. You're giving your life to save your fellow Cypriots."

The man mumbled.

"I can't hear you," Remo said.

The man mumbled again.

25

Remo reached down and removed the man's right elbow from his mouth.

"Talk up now. What'd you say?"

"To hell with fellow Cypriots," the man said.

"That's what I'd thought you'd say," Remo said. "If I meet any more, I'll pass on the message."

And then he was back out into the cold windy night, moving smoothly across the snow back toward the icy cliff.

Yes, that's what he was, he was a man. Remo Williams smiled. Sometimes that wasn't a bad thing to be.

When he got back to the houseboat on Lake Winnepesaukee, that illusion was shattered. He learned that he had two left feet and compared with him, hippopotamuses were ballet dancers and an elephant trumpeting was a whisper and "I don't know why I let you hang around with me."

Remo had changed from his black mesh suit into black chinos and a white tee shirt. He lifted his head up from the built-in couch on the houseboat and looked at the old Oriental who had spoken.

The man was sitting on the indoor-outdoor rugging of the floor. He was surrounded by inkwells and quill pens and on his lap, he had a large sheet of parchment. Behind him were a half dozen more sheets.

All the sheets, including the one on his lap, were blank.

"Can't write again today, huh, Chiun?" Remo said.

"I could write anytime I wanted," Chiun said, "if my heart were not so heavy."

Remo turned away and looked out the window

over his head. The stars still twinkled in the night-time sky but already the horizon was lightening as dawn grew near. Without looking back, Remo said:

"I suppose you better tell me how I'm ruining your life this time."

"You are very cooperative," Chiun said.

"Just thoughtful," said Remo. "I'm a thoughtful man. I figured that out tonight on the mountain. I'm a man. Nothing else. All your silly Korean legends about Shiva, the Destroyer, and me being a god are all just that. Hogwash. I'm a man."

"Hah," said Chiun. "Thoughtful, you say." His voice was a high pitched piping and his English was precise and unaccented. "It is to laugh. You. Thoughtful. It is to laugh. Heh, heh, heh, heh, heh."

"Yes, thoughtful," said Remo. "Because if I don't let you blame whatever it is you want to blame on me, then you'd have to face up to the fact that you just can't write a thing."

"I do not believe I am hearing this," Chiun said.

"Just what I said," Remo said. "Not a word. You can't write movies and you can't write books and you can't write stories and now, even when you conned some magazine guy into publishing it, you can't even write that icky-poo Ung poetry of yours. And God knows anybody can write that."

"Easily said," said Chiun. "How empty are children's boasts."

"Ung Poem Number One Thousand Three Hundred and Six," said Remo. "Oh, flower. Oh, flower with petals. Oh, flower with pretty petals. Here comes a bee. It is a big bee. Oh, bee, see the flower. Oh, flower, see the bee. Open, flower. Accept the bee. Fly fast, bee, and greet the flower."

"Enough," screamed Chiun. "Enough." He rose to his feet in a flash like steam suddenly released from a kettle. He was a small man, barely five feet tall, and his yellow skin was wrinkled with the age of eighty years. His yellow brocaded robe swirled about his body, and his hazel eyes glared at Remo.

"More than enough," Remo said. "It's crap. Anybody can do it. Want to hear another one?"

"No one can write with these distractions," Chiun said.

"Anybody can write Ung poetry. Anytime," Remo said. "The only thing that's kept it from being the laughing stock of the world for two thousand years is that it's written in Korean and nobody can understand how bad it is."

"I do not understand how someone can start a conversation so agreeably and turn so perverse so quickly," Chiun said. "All you white people are crazy but you are an exceptional specimen."

"That's right," Remo said. "I forgot. I was going to let you blame it all on me how you couldn't write. Go ahead. What was it, Little Father? My breathing. I was breathing too loud."

"No," said Chiun. "Your breathing was no noisier than it always is. The snorting of a warthog."

"What then? My muscles. You heard them rippling and the rhythm was wrong, right?"

"Wrong. Not your muscles," said Chiun.

"What then?" demanded Remo.

"Where were you tonight?" asked Chiun. His voice was soft and Remo was immediately wary.

"You know where I was. I had to go up the mountain and take care of those bomb-throwers."

"And where was I?" asked Chiun.

28

Remo shrugged. "I don't know. Here, I guess."

"That's just it," Chiun said. "You go out all the time, and I stay here. All by myself."

Remo sat up. "Wait a minute, Chiun. Let me get this straight. You want to go out on jobs with me?"

"Maybe," said Chiun. "I'd like to be asked."

"I thought you liked to be alone," Remo said.

"Sometimes I do."

"I got this place just so that you could be alone and write," Remo said.

"Snow is depressing. I can't write when it snows."

"We'll go someplace warm. Florida. Miami's warm."

"The old women in Miami talk too much about their sons, the doctors. All I can talk about is you."

"Chiun, what do you want?"

"That is what I want," Chiun said.

"What is?"

"I want you to ask me once in a while what I want. Maybe some times I would like to go out on assignment. I would like to be considered as a person with feelings, not a piece of furniture that one leaves when one goes out, knowing that it will be there when he returns."

"All right, Chiun. From now on, I'll ask."

"Good," said Chiun. He began to pick up his parchment, pens, and ink from the floor. "I'll put this away."

He stashed all the equipment in a large orange lacquered trunk, one of fourteen placed against the walls of the houseboat.

"Remo," he said as he leaned over the trunk.

"What, Little Father?"

"Dr. Smith hired me to train you, correct?"

29

"Correct."

"Nothing was said about my going out on missions, correct?"

"Correct."

"Therefore if I go out on missions, it would seem the tribute should be renegotiated."

"Not a chance," Remo said. "Smitty'd go through the roof. He already delivers enough gold to that village of yours to run a South American country."

"A small country," Chiun said.

"No raise. He'll never go for it."

"Suppose you ask him," suggested Chiun.

Remo shook his head. "He thinks I spend too much as it is."

"Suppose I offer to stay within the President's guidelines for noninflationary wage increases," Chiun said.

"Try it. What've you got to lose?"

"You think he will increase the tribute?"

"No," said Remo.

"I will try anyway," Chiun said. He closed the trunk lid and stood looking out across the dark waters of the lake. Both men were silent and then Remo began to laugh.

"What do you find humorous?" Chiun asked.

"We forgot something," Remo said.

"What did we forget?" Chiun said.

"Smitty doesn't negotiate contracts any more."

"No? Who does?"

"Ruby Gonzalez," said Remo.

Chiun wheeled about and looked at Remo, searching his face for truth. Remo nodded. Chiun groaned.

"Oh, woe is me," he said.

CHAPTER THREE

The fourteen Japanese businessmen were ready. Each of them had admired the suits of the other thirteen. Each of them had passed out thirteen of his own business cards and received back thirteen from the other men, all of whom knew each other well. Each of them paused to admire either the printing or the card stock of each business card, and sometimes both.

Nine of them had carried cameras and had insisted upon taking pictures of all the others, arranged in as many combinations and permutations as was possible. Three of them had shown off their new tape recorders installed in their attache cases, along with their cordless telephones, their new micro-chip printed circuit information processors, and their print-out calculators.

Finally they were seated, waiting. They talked politely among themselves, even as they glanced at their gold LCD watches, wondering why Elmer Lippincott Jr. was late for the meeting, particularly since he had asked them to the secret meeting and particularly since all the men at the table knew its purpose was to use Japanese intermediaries to open up vast new trade contacts between the United States and Red

China, in order to shore up the American dollar, which had been taking an international pasting for two years.

All the businessmen had been advised by the Japanese Trade Council that Lem Lippincott had met only two weeks earlier with the President of the United States, and so all knew what the meeting was about, and they were surprised he was late.

Around the table, the times on the LCD watches ranged from five minutes and twenty seconds after eleven to five minutes and twenty-seven seconds after eleven.

Mariko Kakirano said mildly in Japanese: "I wish he would hurry. I have other pressing business."

There were thirteen nods of agreement, and all looked toward the door of the oak-panelled board room of the Ginza Bank, Tokyo's largest.

"I'm sure he will be here shortly," said another businessman. Thirteen faces turned to him as he spoke and nodded agreement when he was finished.

In a small conference room twenty feet away from where the Japanese businessmen sat, Lem Lippincott was having a different thought.

"I don't want to go," he told his secretary. Lippincott rubbed his fingertips up and down along his smoothly shaven pink cheek.

"I don't understand, sir," said his secretary, a young man who wore a black suit, white shirt and black tie so naturally that it looked as if he had been born in a morgue.

"Nothing to understand," said Lippincott. "I just don't want to go. I don't feel like it. Something doesn't feel right."

He stood up. He was a tall man, the only one of

the three Lippincott sons to be tall like their father, but unlike his father, whose rail-lean figure still looked like the body of an oilfield roustabout, Lem Lippincott had a big soft belly and a wide behind.

He walked to the window and looked down on the teeming street, then turned away quickly as if he had seen something he didn't like.

His secretary was worried. Lippincott had insisted upon being flown into Japan in a private airplane. He had insisted upon being driven to the hotel room from the airport in an American car, driven by an American. And he had literally sneaked into the hotel through a back entrance, first sending the driver up to make sure he would not meet any hotel personnel on the way. Once in his room, Lippincott had given his secretary instructions that he wanted no maids to come into his room.

"But your bed, sir?"

"I'll make my own damn bed," Lippincott had said.

They had left the hotel for the morning meeting the same way. Down a back elevator, into a waiting car with curtains over the windows, and up a back flight of steps to this meeting room.

It occurred to Lippincott's secretary that the American businessman had been in Tokyo nearly twelve hours and had not yet seen a Japanese.

Lippincott paced the delicate patterned rug in the small room like a caged animal. He rubbed his hands together over and over, as if washing them of some infinitesimal speck of dirt.

"I hate this yellow rug," he said. "They got small rugs in this country. Small, yellow rugs. Everything small and yellow. You're not getting enough sun, Gerald, you're getting pasty."

The secretary sighed under his breath. Breakdown.

"I'll tell them that you've been taken ill, sir," he said.

Lippincott looked up as if, for the first time, realizing that his secretary was in the room.

He shook his head.

"No, no, that'll never do. Don't you know, boy, we Lippincotts never get ill. Father wouldn't hear of it. We'll go to your freaking meeting. Let's just get it over with fast."

As they walked down the short hallway to the conference room, Lippincott leaned next to his secretary and whispered, "Stay close to me. I may need you."

The secretary nodded, even as he wondered what Lippincott meant.

He stepped ahead of the taller man to open the door to the conference room, then moved aside to let Lippincott go in first.

The fourteen Japanese businessmen, as they saw Lippincott in the doorway, rose to their feet as a sign of respect.

The secretary saw the American recoil a step, as if expecting an assault on his person.

Lippincott froze there a moment and the secretary walked around in front of him into the room.

"Thank you, gentlemen," he said. "Will you please be seated?"

The fourteen men sat down. The secretary turned to Lippincott and smiled at him, as if to reassure him. Lippincott nodded, but came into the room slowly, seemingly searching for land mines.

He came to the end of the table nearest the door and pulled the chair out. He pulled it four feet from the table, turned it sideways and then sat on the edge of it. It was as if he was expecting to have to make a dash for the door at any moment and this would give him the biggest headstart. The Japanese looked at him with polite curiosity. Mariko Kakirano stood up at the table and moved his chair four feet from the table too, then sat down again. The other thirteen businessmen did the same. To get something from their attache cases now, they would have to stand and walk to the table.

The secretary saw beads of sweat appear on the Lippincott forehead. The businessman hissed to him:

"Gerald, you get a chair. Sit between me and them."

Definitely a breakdown, the secretary thought. Unless he was very mistaken, Lem Lippincott would soon be spending some time at the ha-ha house.

The Japanese sat quietly, smiling, until Gerald was seated. He put his chair halfway between Lippincott and the table, but at an angle so he could watch both the Japanese and Lippincott. The American businessman was sweating now like a marathon runner, looking around the room, from yellow face to yellow face. Was he searching for someone? Or something? the secretary wondered.

Lippincott opened his mouth to speak.

Each word seemed to be a labor to produce.

"You gentlemen know why we're here," Lippincott said haltingly, a pause between each word.

There were fourteen nods at the table.

"The President wants the Lippincott companies, through your companies, to open up trade with Red

35

China, as a way of increasing trade and helping the dollar. That's what he thinks."

Fourteen more nods.

"I know better," Lippincott said. His speech was speeding up.

"I know you little yellow devils can't be trusted," Lippincott said. "You think I forgot Pearl Harbor?"

The secretary looked in shock at Lippincott and then around the table. There were stunned looks on the Japanese faces, then murmurs of protest.

"Don't argue with me, you heathen midgets," Lippincott said. "I know what you're like. Trying to catch us unawares, trying to do us in. When you and those Chinks get together, the first thing you'll do is try to figure out how you can pick on our flesh." Lippincott's knuckles were white where he gripped the arms of the chair.

Mariko Kakirano rose in his chair. "Mr. Lippincott, I must protest."

Before he could say anything more, Lippincott shrunk back in his chair. "Stay away from me, you. I'm warning you. Stay away from me. No more Bataan death marches. Remember Corregidor." He cringed like a child waiting to be struck.

"You have no right," Kakirano said.

The thirteen other businessmen rose to their feet, too. Some of their faces were angry. Most were just startled or confused.

But before Kakirano could say any more, Lem Lippincott jumped to his feet. He put his hands out in front of him, as if warding off invisible blows from the fourteen men standing in front of him.

"No, you don't, you yellow devils. I know what

you're after, trying to pick my bones, eat my flesh. You won't get away with it."

The secretary rose. Lippincott was waving his arms in front of him, fighting imaginary hordes of insects.

"Sir," the secretary said, "I think we'd better . . ."

Before he could finish his sentence, one of Lippincott's flailing arms caught him alongside the head and knocked him back into his chair.

"You too, eh? In league with these vultures."

Mariko Kakirano shook his head in disgust. He glanced around the table. The other men nodded to him. Kakirano took a step toward the door, and the other men moved from their chairs, and lined up behind him in a neat single file.

"Coming after me, eh? You won't get me," Lippincott shouted. He turned away and ran. His left leg knocked against his secretary's chair, spilling it over and dumping the young man onto the carpet. He rolled to a sitting position and looked after Lippincott, just in time to see the businessman dive headfirst through the plate glass window and extend his arms in a swandive toward the street, four stories below.

Lem Lippincott did not go alone. His plunging body crashed into three elderly Japanese as it hit the crowded sidewalk. All four were killed.

The Tokyo police, after careful investigation, called it a tragic accident.

Later that day, the telephone rang in the office of Dr. Elena Gladstone, director of Lifeline Laboratory. The telephone sounded with an electronic beep, instead of the usual ringing bell. Before answering it,

Dr. Gladstone pressed a button under her desk, which double-locked her office door.

"Yes," she said as she picked up the phone, then listened to a voice that explained what had happened to Lem Lippincott.

"Oh, I'm sorry," she said.

"I didn't want him dead," the voice said.

"You can't always tell how someone will react," she said. "This is all very experimental."

"Don't let anything like that happen again," the voice said.

"I won't," she promised, as she replaced the receiver, but with the phone hung up and behind the privacy of her locked office door, Dr. Gladstone put back her head and laughed aloud.

Twenty-five miles north of Dr. Gladstone's Manhattan office, another telephone rang that afternoon.

Dr. Harold W. Smith, head of the secret agency known as CURE, took the receiver from the bottom left drawer of his desk, and spun around in his chair so he could look through the one-way windows out over Long Island Sound.

"Yes, sir," he said.

Smith had run the secret agency through five Presidents and each had a different character on the telephone. The agency had been set up by the first of those five, a young President who had met an assassin's bullet. He had designed CURE intentionally to work independently of the White House. A President could not assign CURE or its personnel. He could only suggest missions. The single order a President could give to Smith would be for CURE to disband. In choosing Smith to head the organization, that first

President had picked wisely because Smith was one man who would disband the organization immediately upon receiving such an order, without any regard for his own life or that of anyone else. It was a sign of what America had gone through in the sixties and seventies that every President had wanted to disband CURE but none had ever given that order.

Smith knew all their voices. The brittle, clipped New England accent that made its mispronunciations sound like a planned virtue; the earthy Texas drawl that was the sound of a man who lived close to the soil and whose emotions lived close to the surface, the most truly alive of all the Presidents Smith had known. There was the California sharpness of the voice of the next President, a voice that always sounded as if it had everything planned and organized in advance; that sounded as if it had considered twenty-five things it might say and rejected twenty-four and seized upon the best. It was a voice that sounded professional and precise and Smith always had the feeling that under it was a man held on such a tight string that if any part of it every loosened, the entire man would come apart. That voice was followed by another, a halting flat Midwestern voice. The President who spoke like that seemed to have no feel for the English language and gave no sense that he had any idea what he was talking about. But his instincts had been sound and his heart was strong. Smith had liked him. He couldn't speak but he could lead.

It was a mark of Smith's character that he had not voted for a President in eighteen years. He thought choosing between one candidate or another might, in some small way, influence him when dealing with whichever man became President. So he hadn't voted for this new President and had never even considered whether he would have or not. But he allowed himself the occasional luxury of admitting to himself that he did not like the man. The President was a Southerner and Smith recognized that he was prejudiced against him, thought about him primarily in terms of how the man's voice sounded over the telephone. His voice wasn't melodic, the way many Southern voices were. This voice was choppy, pausing at the wrong time, as if reading groups of words selected at random. And while the man was a trained scientist, he seemed to Smith to be continuously fighting to overcome the possibility that the scientific method might have any influence in his life. He had an inordinate capacity for fooling himself and seeing things that weren't there, and Smith realized that not only did he dislike the man, but he was displeased with himself for not being able to figure the President out more clearly.

But he put his personal feelings toward the President of the United States aside as he answered the telephone.

"What do you know about the Lippincott case?" the Southern voice asked.

"I received the reports on what actually happened in Tokyo," Smith said. "I have investigated and found them accurate. I did a cursory probe and turned up nothing. No problems in Mr. Lippincott's home life or business. No record of mental illness, no record of hospitalization or private treatment or whatever," said Smith. At this time, Lem Lippincott had been dead eight hours. "So I would tend toward the conclusion that it was a total, unpredictable, and tragic breakdown. The man just snapped under some kind of pressure."

"I thought that too," said the President, "but just a few minutes ago, this very unusual letter came across my desk."

"Letter? From whom?" asked Smith.

The President sighed. "I wish I knew. It's just a rambling, disjointed kind of thing that doesn't make a lot of sense."

"It sounds like much of your mail," Smith said drily.

"Yes, it does," the President said. "Usually it would have been thrown right out and I never would have seen it, but this happened to hang around and somebody showed it to me after we heard about Lippincott. And I thought it might be important."

"What does it say, sir?" Smith asked, trying to hide his impatience. He hooked the telephone onto his shoulder and carefully tightened the knot of his regimental striped tie.

Smith was a tall spare man, now in his sixties and going bald. He wore a gray suit and vest with an unwrinkled familiarity that made it clear he had worn that costume all his life. More and more his looks had began to symbolize the rocky New England he came from, a look that seemed always to have been old.

"It's about the Lippincotts," the President's voice said. "It says there's a plot to kill them all and it has something to do with animals."

"Animals, sir? What has it to do with animals?"

"The damned letter doesn't say."

"Does it say who is behind this so-called plot?"

"No, it doesn't say that either."

"What does it say?"

"It says that the writer is a New York City private detective."

"Name," asked Smith as he reached down and tapped a button under his desk. A panel in the center of the desk moved and a computer console rose silently. Smith was ready to tap the name into it, even while the President spoke, to get the giant computer banks of CURE, the largest computer banks in the world, on the trail of the private detective.

"There is no name," the President said.

Smith sighed. "I see. What does it say?"

"It says the writer is a New York City detective. He knows that there is a plot to kill the Lippincotts. It has something to do with animals and he doesn't know what. But he is going to find out. It says that when the Lippincotts aren't killed then I'll know he was telling the truth and he'll be in touch with me about giving him a medal."

"That doesn't make much sense," Smith said.

"No, it doesn't," the President agreed. "But that incident with Lem Lippincott . . . well, it made me wonder."

Smith nodded. Far out on the sound, he saw a sailboat whipped along by the wind and wondered who would be out sailing on a cold wintry day like this one.

"It seems clear," he said, "that you should turn the letter over to the Lippincott family. They have the resources to protect themselves."

"I know that. But the fact is, Dr. Smith, that we can't afford the possibility of this letter being right."

"Why not?"

"Because I asked the Lippincott family to work

out a number of overseas proposals. They look like simple business deals but the idea was to use the Lippincott resources and work through companies in Japan to open up major new trading markets in Red China."

"And you think some foreign power might be trying to prevent that?" asked Smith.

"It's a possibility," the President said.

"I wish I had known this before," Smith said. "We could have taken steps to protect Lem Lippincott when he went to Tokyo."

"I know, I know," the President said. "But I didn't envision any trouble. I thought it would just move smoothly along like any other business deal."

Smith resisted the impulse to lecture the President on all the international efforts being made by the Communist bloc in boardrooms and bank offices around the world to try to undermine the United States' economy. No one in his right mind, except the most feather-brained kind of dreamer, should have expected a major attempt to bolster the dollar to go unnoticed and fail to draw a response from the people in the world who would rejoice at the dollar's destruction. But all the politicians Smith had known lived in a perpetual world where hope always triumphed over reason, good wishes over historical lessons. So he said nothing.

"I think your people should get on this," the President said.

"Yes, sir. I'll need the letter."

"You'll be using those two, I suppose?

"I imagine so," Smith said. "Even though they are not designed to function as bodyguards."

"Tell them to be circumspect," the President said.

"All the killings . . ."

Smith remembered how Remo and Chiun had saved this President's life from an assassination attempt; how they had headed off World War III when a member of the President's inner circle of friends had unwittingly unleashed a murder attempt on the Russian premier. His New England heart could characterize the President's statement as nothing more than ingratitude.

He tried to keep the edge out of his voice when he said: "If you'd rather I didn't use them . . . I'm sure they can find other things to do."

"No, no," the President said quickly. "Just tell them to keep the deaths down."

"One does not tell them what to do or how to do it," Smith said coldly. "One gives them an assignment, and then stands out of the way. Should I assign them, yes or no?"

"Yes," the President said. "Whatever you say."

"No, sir," said Smith. "It's what you say."

The letter from the President was in Smith's hands in ninety minutes. When Smith read it, he marvelled that someone could have used up three pages of legal sized yellow paper and written such a little amount of information. There was no name and address of the writer, and there was a brief mention of a plot to kill all the Lippincott family and that it had something to do with trained animals. The rest of the letter complained about Italian jockeys, policemen on the take, and the high cost of Fleischmann's Rye whiskey.

If a Lippincott had not died by willingly diving headfirst out a Tokyo window, the letter would have been consigned immediately to a trash basket.

Smith pressed a button on the right hand side of

his telephone receiver and a moment later a woman entered his office.

She was a tall black woman with skin the color of whipped coffee mocha. She wore a pair of leather trousers and a tan tweed blazer with matching leather patches on the elbows. A moderate Afro crowned her head. She was not truly beautiful but her eyes twinkled with intelligence and when she smiled, as she did now at Smith, it was more than a social gesture, it was an act of warmth.

Her name was Ruby Jackson Gonzalez and she served as Smith's administrative assistant. She had been a CIA agent, but on two separate occasions she had been drawn into the orbit of Remo and Chiun. In the process she had figured out enough about CURE to make her a candidate for killing or hiring. She carefully eliminated the first possibility by black-mailing Smith with a well-planned threat of exposure and so he was forced to hire her. She was organized, earthy, and smart and she had another virtue as well. When she wanted to, her voice could rise in pitch high enough and loud enough to crack granite, and she used her voice as a weapon to keep Remo in line. He would do anything Smith wanted just as long as Ruby didn't yell at him.

Chiun also had a special feeling for Ruby. He thought if that if she and Remo had a baby, it wouldn't be yellow, which was a proper color, but it would be tan, which was close enough, and Chiun could take it young and train it properly to be a Master of Sinanju, something he bitterly complained he could not do with Remo because he got to him too late. Chiun had offered many gold pieces to Ruby if she would just do this little thing for him. Ruby said there were some things she was not prepared to do for money. Remo said that was merely a bargaining ploy to get Chiun to raise his price.

Ruby was convinced that if she wanted Remo, she'd have him. Anytime, anywhere. Remo, for his part, was sure that all it would take would be a snap of the fingers and Ruby would be his slave for life.

Ruby Jackson Gonzalez had also killed a half dozen men. She was twenty-three years old.

"Yes, sir," she told Smith.

He handed her the letter and she glanced at it quickly.

"I want you to find the writer."

She looked up from the hugely scrawled writing on the yellow sheets.

"What asylum should I look in first?" she asked. When she saw that Smith did not think that was funny, she said "Right away."

She took the letter to her small private office outside Smith's where she was the only other person in CURE to have a computer console and access to the giant memories of the organization's electronic brain.

She punched up the computer console, then spread the three pages of the note side by side by side on her desk to examine. The sprawling, semi-literate handwriting might be her best bet and she asked the computer to reproduce for her the signatures from the license applications of all the private detectives in New York City.

The machine sat silently, as it scoured its banks for three minutes, and then on photo sensitive paper which clicked out of the top of Ruby's console, it began to spin out samples of the signature and, next to them, the printed names of all the private detectives in New York.

There were hundreds of them and they came out on a big reel of paper from the back of the console. Ruby looked at them carefully. The samples of handwriting were small, hardly enough for a perfect analysis, but she narrowed the long string of names down to ten. She also reminded herself that there were ten illiterate detectives in New York City whom she would never hire under any circumstances.

Ruby looked at the letter again and smiled to herself when she read the diatribe against Italian jockeys. On instinct, she punched in the ten names of possible suspects into the machine and asked the computer to cross-check them against telephone accounts with New York's Off-Track Betting office.

The computer narrowed it down to three names. Ed Kolle. J. R. DeRose. Zack Meadows.

She checked the samples of the three men's signatures against the note again, but was unable to tell which of them might have written it. All of them seemed to have gone to the same school to learn illegibility.

She read over the note again, finally fixing on a paragraph that read: "And when you start doing something in the white house, don't you think you ought to do something about cops on the take, and corruption cops who take a piece out of everything and shake down everybody whether they deserves it or not."

On another hunch, she punched the three names into the computer and asked it to check the names against applicants during the past twenty years for

47

the New York City police department. The machine searched for another three minutes and then gave Ruby back one name.

Zack Meadows.

Ruby took out a Manhattan telephone book and called the office of Zack Meadows. She recognized its location as a seedy section on the west side, a rollicking dirty slum.

The telephone had been disconnected. She asked the computer why.

It patched itself into the computers of New York Bell system and reported back that the phone service had been shut off for nonpayment of bill.

Ruby asked the computer for a full background on Zack Meadows. It gave back his home address (a slum); his military record (undistinguished); his educational background (sparse); and his income tax records (laughable).

There was no home telephone listing, but Ruby got the address of the apartment house superintendent from a reverse telephone directory, called him and found out that Meadows had not been seen in two weeks and his rent was four days overdue.

Enough.

The letter had been written by Zack Meadows. And Zack Meadows had been among the missing for the last few weeks.

She went back into Smith's office.

"His name is Zack Meadows. He ain't been seen in three weeks."

Smith nodded and thought for a moment.

He said, "I'm sending you to New York."

"Good. My ass be dragging hanging out at my

48

desk all the time. You want me to look for this Meadows?"

"Yes," said Smith. "This is why." He filled her in quickly on the threat to the Lippincotts and what it might mean to America's economy if there was a full-scale threat against the family.

"Got it," said Ruby. "I'll leave right away."

She turned for the door. Smith said, "Also, arrange a meeting for me with Remo."

"When?" Ruby asked.

"As soon as possible."

"Okay. Tonight," she said.

"It'll never be tonight," Smith said.

"Why not?" asked Ruby.

"Remo likes more notice than that. He won't show up."

"He'll be there," Ruby said. "You can bank on it."

At the door, she turned back. "You putting him on this too?" she asked.

Smith nodded.

"Tell that turkey I said I'll find out what it's about before he does."

CHAPTER FOUR

Remo glared at Smith.

"You want us to do what?"

Chiun said, "He just told you he wants us to guard the Lippincott family."

"I heard him," Remo growled.

"Then why did you ask him to repeat himself?"

"Because I wanted him to say it again is all," Remo said.

"I see," Chiun said. "That makes it all clear." He rolled his eyes upward in his head and turned toward the window in the fourteenth floor suite in the Meadowlands Hilton. Across the narrow strip of the Hackensack River and a buffer zone of New Jersey meadowlands, he could see darkened Giants Stadium where other teams came in and did football to the Giants. Next to it was the brightly-lighted Meadowlands racetrack, its lights glowing in the dim foggy night like the radium smear in Madame Curie's saucer.

"Why?" Remo asked Smith. "If the Lippincotts need guarding, they got enough money to hire the Pinkertons. All the Pinkertons. Throw in the FBI too, for good measure."

Smith shook his head. He was used to these complaints. "We don't know that, Remo," he said.

"Why not?"

"Because we don't know who is behind this attempt to kill the Lippincotts. If there is one."

"You better start at the top," Remo said. "You're confusing me more than you usually do."

"I find it perfectly clear," Chiun said.

Smith said, "One of the Lippincotts dove out a window in Tokyo. Nobody knows it but he was there on a special trade mission for the President. The President got word that someone was going to kill all the Lippincotts, using animals somehow. We don't know what that was about."

"You know a lot," Remo said.

Smith continued. "It's just possible that a foreign government may be trying to do in the Lippincott family so they can't perform this special mission for the President. We don't know but we can't take chances. That's why we need you."

"What's this big special mission the Lippincotts were on?" Remo asked.

"It has to do with currency and the dollar abroad," Smith said.

"No more," Remo said. "I hate economics."

"I find it very interesting," said Chiun, turning back to the room. "You may tell me."

"You would find it interesting," Remo said.

Smith nodded and began explaining to Chiun about the declining value of the dollar and how it raised the prices Americans paid for imports and how these higher prices brought about higher prices on American goods. These higher prices brought about higher wages, with no increase in productivity, and this caused inflation and inflation, through a series of steps, caused joblessness and joblessness threatened to cause depression.

As he spoke, Remo sat down on the edge of the couch and with his hands, spun the cylinder of an imaginary revolver, opened it, inserted an imaginary bullet, closed the cylinder, spun it again, put the imaginary gun to his head, cocked the hammer and squeezed the trigger, blowing his imaginary brains out. His head slumped off to one side. Smith stared at him.

Chiun said to Smith, "Ignore him. He was not allowed outside for recess today."

Remo sat there, his head lolling to one side like a dead man, until Smith had finished.

"I see," said Chiun. "We will guard the Lippincotts because this is very important."

Remo sat upright.

"We will, huh? Who says so?"

"Ruby Gonzalez said you'd be glad to take the assignment," Smith said.

"Well, Ruby's playing with a half a deck," Remo said. "I'm not afraid of her anymore." He reached into his pocket and brought out two little cones of soft surgical rubber. "See these? Earplugs. The next time I see her, I'm just going to slip them in and she can yell all she wants for all I care and it won't do her any good. Where is Ruby anyway?"

"She's working on this same case," Smith said. "She's trying to track down the person who wrote that letter to the President about the Lippincotts."

"But where?" asked Remo.

"In New York," Smith said. He waved in the general direction of New York City, only four miles away from the hotel where they sat.

Remo opened a side window and stuck his head out.

"Ruby," he shouted into the night. "I'm not afraid of you anymore."

He cocked his head, as if listening, then came back into the room.

"She said she didn't find out anything yet."

"I didn't hear anything," Smith said.

"It's only four miles," Remo said. "Ruby's whisper can carry four miles."

"But she is a nice lady," Chiun said. "She will give you wonderful children."

"Not on your life, Chiun," said Remo.

"That's true," Chiun said. He confided to Smith in a stage whisper, "Ruby will not have him. She has told me many times that she considers Remo too ugly to father her child."

"Yeah?" said Remo.

"Ruby said something else," said Smith. "Let me get this just right. She said to tell the turkey that she would find out what this is all about before he did."

"She did, huh?" demanded Remo.

Smith nodded. "Elmer Lippincott Sr. is at his estate in White Plains. He is expecting you. He has been told that you are consultants with the government and are setting up new security procedures for the family. And if you keep in touch, I'll let you know what Ruby finds out."

"We won't need that," Remo said. "We'll have this cleaned up before she finds a place to park her car."

After Smith had left, Remo said to Chiun "I still think it's stupid, Little Father. Guarding the Lippincotts. We're not bodyguards. Let them hire their own."

"You're absolutely right," Chiun said.

"Wait a minute. Wait a minute. Say that again," Remo said.

"You're absolutely right. Why say it again?"

"I wanted to savor it," said Remo. "If I'm absolutely right, why are we doing this?"

"It's very simple," Chiun said. "You heard Emperor Smith. If we do this, it will save America a lot of dollars. It seems only correct that if we save America many dollars, some of them should come to us."

"That's not what Smith meant when he was talking about saving the dollar," Remo said.

"It's not?" asked Chiun.

"No."

"Oh, the duplicity of the man," said Chiun. "Remo, through the course of history, the House of Sinanju has worked for many emperors, but this is the only one who never says what he means, and always means something different from what he says."

"You're right," said Remo. "But we're going to do it anyway."

"Why?"

"To teach Ruby a lesson," Remo said. He went back to the open window and leaned out.

"Ruby," he shouted. "You hear me? We're coming."

A voice from six stories down answered back. "Hey, fella, shut up. We got a game this week." It was a deep Texas voice.

"Get lost," Remo said.

"What's that, fella? What's that?"

"Are you as deaf as you are dumb?" Remo asked. "I said, get lost."

"What room you in, fella?"

"And your cheerleaders are ugly," Remo said.

"What room?" the man shouted.

"Room fourteen-twenty-two. Bring your friends," Remo said.

And so it was that the stage was set for the football Giants to win their first game of the year when the entire starting defensive team of the Dallas Cowboys came down with a serious illness two days before the game. The ton-and-a-half of players decided to tell the coach they were sick, rather than try to get him to believe the truth, which was that they accosted an ancient Oriental and a skinny white man in the fourteenth floor hallway of the Meadowlands Hilton, and were tossed around the hallway like bowling pins. The Giants, given the privilege of playing against Dallas's defensive second string, ran wild, managed to score nine points on three field goals and won 9–8, surrendering the eight points when their own quarterbacks were tackled four times in the Giant's end zone while trying off-tackle plays on third and twenty.

Remo and Chiun did not see the game. They were in New York.

CHAPTER FIVE

Elmer Lippincott Sr. slid quietly out of his giant king-sized bed, moving slowly so he would not wake his wife Gloria who slept next to him. Lippincott was eighty years old, a tall spare man with a face that had been weathered and hardened by an early life spent in the search for oil in the deserts of the world, in Texas, Iran, and Saudi Arabia, and in the steaming jungles of South America.

He moved with a smooth vigor that belied his years. His face was perpetually ruddy and his hair a shock of thick white wool. If his blue eyes had had more twinkle, he might have looked like an Irish saloon keeper who had gone on the wagon twenty years earlier. But Elmer Lippincott's eyes were flint hard and piercing. They softened now, however, as he stood next to the bed and looked down at his wife who slept on undisturbed. Gloria Lippincott was a young blonde woman, in her mid-twenties, and her skin was as soft and creamy as Lippincott's was tough and leathery.

Her long blonde hair displayed itself around her head on the pillow like a golden frame, and the old man's heart skipped a little as it always did when he absorbed her beauty when she was not watching. He looked at the blonde hair, the perfect complexion, the long line of her throat, the faint swell below the collarbone. He let his eyes trail down her body and he smiled as he saw the large rounded mound of her stomach under the blue satin sheet. Her belly was big and ripe with his baby. Six months pregnant and, God, she was beautiful.

He touched her belly once, gently, letting his hand linger for a few seconds but there was no answering kick from inside, and disappointed he withdrew his hand. Then he walked quietly from the bedroom into the large dressing room adjoining it.

He spurned a valet.

"I dressed myself all my life. Just because I found some oil don't mean I forgot how to button my own buttons," he had once told an interviewer.

He glanced at his watch. It was exactly 6:30 A.M.

He passed through the kitchen on his way to his downstairs office. Gertie, who had come to him as a young woman and was now in her sixties, stood before a frying pan at the range, and he slapped her roubstly on the butt.

"Morning, Gert," he said loudly.

"Morning, the First," she said without turning. "Your juice is on the tray. So's your coffee."

"Where's my eggs?"

"Hold your horses, they're coming." She flipped the eggs hard enough to break the yolks and while they cooked dry, she pulled two slices of toast from the toaster and spread them with corn oil margarine.

"It's a great day, Gertie," said Lippincott as he drained his six ounces of orange juice in one long gulp.

"You oughta be ashamed of yourself. Lem barely in his grave and you say it's a great day."

Lippincott was chastened. "All right," he said, "so it's not a great day for him. But we're alive and that's a great day. My wife is having my baby and that's a great day. And you're cooking me the finest pair of over dry eggs the world has ever seen and how could that make anything but a great day? A little sadness should never ruin a great day."

"Missie Mary'd be spinning in her grave, she hear you carrying on that way, with Lem dead," said Gertie, disapprovingly, as she scooped the eggs from the skillet and slid them onto a plate, along with three sausage patties she had fried in a separate pan.

"Yes, she probably would," Lippincott said, thinking for a long distasteful moment of Mary, the stern autocratic woman who had been his wife for thirty years and who had mothered the three sons who bore the Lippincott name. "But there are a lot of things that'd make her spin in her garve," he said.

He scooped up his platter of eggs and patted Gertie on the butt again. He refused to lose his good mood. Balancing his coffee cup and plate in one hand, he walked from the kitchen, down the long hallway of the big old mansion and into his oak-panelled office at the far end of the building.

Even though the family fortune was now measured in eleven digits, lifetime habits aren't easily broken and Lippincott still ate like a man who was afraid of the prospect that he might have to share his food with someone else. So he disposed of breakfast as quickly as possible, then put the plate aside, sipped on the coffee and began reading reports that were stacked neatly by his desk.

Lem was dead. He had been entrusted with the overseas deal to open up trading routes with Red China to help the dollar, but now he was dead.

He shouldn't have died, Lippincott thought. That wasn't the plan.

At 9 A.M., he had his first appointment of the day and as he peeled off his jacket and rolled up his sleeve, Elmer Lippincott Sr. repeated that to his visitor.

"It wasn't the plan that Lem should die," he said. Dr. Elena Gladstone nodded as she prepared a hypodermic syringe.

"It was an unfortunate accident," she said. "That happens sometimes when you're dealing with experimental medicine."

Dr. Gladstone wore a tailored tweed suit and a rust blouse that was open four buttons down from the neck. She carried a well-worn leather doctor's bag and from it she extracted a rubber-capped vial of a clear liquid.

"Perhaps we should halt everything?" she said.

"I don't know," he said. "Maybe."

"It's all right," Dr. Gladstone said. "You can forgive and forget, no one will ever know."

"No, dammit," Lippincott growled. "I'll know. You just be more careful."

Dr. Gladstone nodded. Lippincott extended his arm toward her even as she was withdrawing the vial from her doctor's bag.

She smiled at him. Her white teeth looked like pearls against her lightly-tanned skin and her bright red hair. "Not so anxious," she said. "I have to fill the syringe first. I gather everything is going along well."

Lippincott nodded. "My wife's fine and your associate, Dr. Beers, stays here all the time now to take care of her. It couldn't be better."

"And you?" she asked.

He reached mockingly for her breast. She leaned back and his hand closed on empty air.

"Elena," he said. "I'm randy as a billy goat."

"Not bad for a man your age," she said. She had filled the hypodermic with the clear liquid from the vial.

"Not bad?" he said. "Good. Good for a man any age."

She took his left arm, and wiped the inside of his elbow with a cotton pad saturated in alcohol. As she inserted the tip of the needle, she said:

"Well, just remember, before you go spreading the joy around to every nubile woman in your employ, you're not shooting blanks anymore. Be careful or you'll have more Lippincotts running around than you know what to do with."

"Just one," he said. "Just one will be fine."

He smiled as the needle punctured his skin and he could imagine a glow of health and well-being as the clear liquid was injected into his veins.

Dr. Elena Gladstone injected the fluid slowly, pulled the plunger back out to dilute the fluid with Lippincott's blood, then slowly injected the mixture back into his arm.

"There you are," she said as she withdrew the needle. "Good for another two weeks."

"You know, I just may outlive you," Lippincott said to the woman. He rolled down his sleeve, buttoned his cuff and put his jacket back on.

"Maybe," she said.

61

He carefully buttoned all three buttons of his jacket. Elena Gladstone had nice breasts, he decided. Funny, he hadn't noticed before. And the swell of her hip and the long line of her thigh were something, well, they were something he could do something about. Without attempting to appear casual, he walked to his office door and locked it, once with the button lock, and twice by turning the key.

When he turned back, Dr. Gladstone was smiling at him and she had a wide lovely mouth of beautiful teeth and a warm smile, and a man could do something with a smile like that and she seemed to sense it. She knew what he was thinking because she began to open her rust colored blouse, but before she could, Elmer Lippincott Sr. sped his eighty-year-old body across the room to her, lifted her roughly in his strong arms, and carried her to the blue suede leather couch in his office.

Upstairs in Elmer Lippincott's bedroom, his wife Gloria stirred. She stretched languidly in her sleep, then slowly opened her eyes. She turned to her right, saw that her husband was not in bed, then checked the clock on the small marble table near her bed. She smiled and reached out her hand for a button on the table and pressed it.

Twenty seconds later, a tall dark-haired man with light green eyes entered the bedroom through a side door. He was wearing a tee shirt and blue slacks.

Gloria Lippincott looked at him with expectation. "Lock the doors," she said.

He locked all the bedroom doors, and turned back to her.

"I want an examination, Doctor," she said.

62

"That's why I'm here," said Dr. Jesse Beers with a broad smile.

"An internal," Gloria Lippincott said.

He nodded again.

"As I said. That's why I'm here." As he walked toward her, he began opening his trousers.

Back downstairs, Elmer Lippincott zipped up his trousers and put his jacket back on.

"So that's how young you feel," Dr. Elena Gladstone said. "Mmmmmmmm."

"Exactly," he said. "And I owe it all to clean living, good diet and . . ."

"And a healthy dose of erotic juices from the Lifeline Laboratory," the redhead said. She stood up from the blue couch and smoothed her skirt around her hips.

"I give my money away to every dipshit cause that anybody asks me to donate to," Lippincott said. "Your lab's the first one that ever did me any good."

"Our pleasure," she said.

The intercom buzzer rang on the phone on Lippincott's desk, and he walked quickly over to the receiver.

"Yes," he said.

"I'm thinking of you, dear," said Gloria Lippincott.

"And me of you," said Lippincott. "How do you feel?"

"Fine," his wife said. She giggled slightly.

"What's so funny?" Lippincott asked.

"Dr. Beers. He's giving me an examination."

"Is everything all right?"

"Oh, it's fine. Just fine," Gloria said.

"Swell," said Lippincott. "You be sure to do just what the doctor tells you."

"You can count on that," said Gloria. "Anything he says, I'll do."

"Good, and I'll see you in a little while for lunch."

"Bye, bye," Gloria said as she hung up.

Lippincott returned the phone to the desk.

"That Dr. Beers is a good fella," he told Elena Gladstone. "Always on the job."

"That's what we're paid for," Elena said, looking away from the old man with a smile. She finished buttoning her blouse.

There were guards at the beginning of the long private drive that led to Lippincott's sprawling Westchester estate and there were more guards at the big iron gates set into the twelve-foot high stone walls that bordered the grounds.

When they got close to the house, there were more guards prowling the perimeter of the main building, and inside the front door, there were two more guards.

One called by telephone to Elmer Lippincott's office and was told that Remo and Chiun were allowed to pass. The guard escorted them down the hallway, lined with original Picassos, Miros, and Seurats, with an occasional Cremonesi miniature gouache inserted for balance.

"These are ugly pictures," Chiun said.

"They're priceless works of art," the guard said.

Chiun tossed Remo a glance that said clearly that, at best, the guard was a person of no taste and discernment, and, at worst, might even be insane and therefore should be watched out for.

"They're fine," Remo said. "Especially if you like people with three noses."

"In my village, we had a painter," Chiun said. "Oh, could he paint. When he painted a picture of a wave, it looked just like a wave. And when he painted a picture of a tree, it looked just like the tree. That is art. He got much better when I convinced him to stop wasting his time painting pictures of waves and trees and to do important subjects."

"How many paintings did he do of you, Chiun?" Remo asked.

"Ninety-seven," said Chiun. "But who counts? Would you like one?"

"No," said Remo.

"Perhaps this Mr. Lippincott will want to buy them. What did he pay for this junk?" He looked to the guard.

"That Picasso there cost four hundred fifty thousand dollars," the guard said.

"I do not appreciate your humor," Chiun said.

"Four hundred and fifty thou," the guard said. "That's what it cost."

"Is this true, Remo?"

"Probably."

"For a picture of someone with a head like a pyramid?" said Chiun.

Remo shrugged.

"What should I offer my paintings to this Mr. Lippincott for, Remo?" asked Chiun. "He whispered. "Because to tell the truth, I am running out of space for them."

"Try to get a hundred dollars for the lot," Remo said.

"That is insane," said Chiun.

"Sure it is, but you know how these rich folks throw their money around," said Remo.

Elmer Lippincott was escorting Dr. Elena Gladstone to his office door, when the doorbell rang. "This'll be the two security men from the government. I'll handle it." He leaned close to her ear. "And remember, you be careful."

"I understand," she said.

"Fine." He opened the door for her.

Elena Gladstone stepped out into the hall. Her eyes met Remo's. His eyes were as dark as midnight caves and, involuntarily, she sipped in a puff of breath through open lips. She brushed up against him as she walked by and the smell of her hyacinth perfume filled his senses. She looked away and walked down the hall.

"Come on in," Lippincott told his visitors.

Remo was looking down the hallway after Elena Gladstone. As she turned toward the front door, she glanced back at him and when she saw him watching her, she seemed embarrassed and turned her head resolutely away before walking off.

Remo followed Chiun into the office. The smell of the hyacinth perfume was still in his nostrils.

"Nice looking lady," he told Lippincott.

"She smells like a brewery," Chiun said.

"My personal physician," Lippincott said. He nodded to the guard to return to his station and closed the office door.

"You haven't been sick, have you?" asked Remo.

"No," Lippincott said with a small chuckle. "Just my regular checkup. Sit down. What can I do for you?"

"There are ninety-seven paintings for sale," Chiun said. "All beautiful representations of the visage of the kindest, gentlest, most noble . . ."

"Chiun," interrupted Remo sharply. He lounged in the blue suede sofa, facing Lippincott's desk. The sofa seemed permeated with the scent of the perfume. Chiun stood by one of the windows of the room, looking at Lippincott, who sat smoothly behind his desk. Remo asked:

"You know who we are?"

"I know that you've been sent here by people in very high places to see to our security. I don't know why. I don't know anything about it. I've bean asked to cooperate with you, even though we've been doing a pretty good job of protecting ourselves for as long as I've been alive."

"And your son who practiced swan diving into the street? Could he protect himself, too?" asked Remo.

Lippincott's face reddened and his big hands clenched into tight fists.

"Lem was sick," he said. "He just cracked under the strain."

"Some people in Washington think maybe he was helped to crack," Remo said.

"Not a chance," said Lippincott.

"Enough trivia," said Chiun. "About those paintings . . ."

"Please, Chiun," said Remo. "Not now."

Chiun folded his arms and his hands disappeared into the open flowing sleeves of his blue kimono. He gazed impassively at the ceiling.

"Who's taking over the Japanese deal?" Remo asked.

"My son, Randall. The deal's just got to be tied up."

"Then he's the one we've got to watch," Remo said. "Where do we find him?"

"He lives in New York City," Lippincott said. He mentioned an address in the east sixties. "I'll tell him you're coming."

"Please do that," Remo said.

He stood up. "Are you ready, Little Father?"

"Am I allowed not to talk about these priceless art works that have been in my family for ten or eleven years?" asked Chiun.

"What art works?" Lippincott said.

"Paintings of the most noble, most gentle, most . . ."

"Never mind," Remo told Lippincott. "You wouldn't like them."

He nodded to Chiun to follow him and walked to the door. He stopped and looked back at Lippincott.

"Your son, Lem," Remo said.

"Yes?"

"Did he have any pets?"

"Pets?" Lippincott thought a moment. "No. Why?"

"No contact with animals?" asked Remo.

Lippincott shrugged. "Not that I know of. Why?"

"I don't know," Remo said. "Something about animals maybe involved in his death."

"That might make sense to you," said Lippincott, "but it doesn't make any to me."

"Me neither," Remo agreed. "We'll see you."

He preceded Chiun into the hallway and walked toward the front door. At the top of the broad flight of steps leading toward the second floor, they saw a tall blonde woman wearing a white satin dressing gown, her stomach swelled with the child she was bearing. She smiled down at them, before walking away.

"There is something I do not understand," Chiun said.

"What's that?" asked Remo.

"I do not understand how there come to be so many Americans."

"What?" asked Remo.

"That is the first women with child I have seen in this country in more than a year."

Remo wasn't listening. At the front door, he asked the guard:

"Who's the blonde?"

"Mrs. Lippincott."

"What Mrs. Lippincott?"

"Mrs. Elmer Lippincott Sr."

Remo winked to the guard. "No wonder the old man keeps looking so fit."

The guard nodded. "You better believe it."

Behind his locked office door, Elmer Lippincott was directing the mobile operator to contact the car of Elena Gladstone.

When she came on the air, he said "Those two men. They wanted to know something about animals."

"I see," said Elena Gladstone after a pause.

"Perhaps things should cool down for a while."

"Leave it with me," she said. She replaced the receiver in the console of her silver Jaguar XJ-12. In

her mind's eye, she saw the two men outside Lippincott's office. The old Oriental and the young American with the piercing eyes and the smooth movements of an athlete. No, it wasn't an athlete. The
movements didn't look so much like power as they
did like grace. Perhaps, like a ballet dancer. She
hoped she saw them again. Especially the young one.

She parked her car in the public garage next to the
Lifeline Laboratory, walked into her building and
went straight to her private office.

She made two telephone calls.

On the first, she quickly recounted that two government agents were interested. "I think the old
man's getting cold feet," she said. "About Randall."

She got a two-word reply.

"Kill him."

"But the old man?" she said.

"I'll take care of him."

She nodded as the phone clicked in her ear.

Her next telephone call was to the headquarters of
the Lippincott National Bank, into the private office
of Randall Lippincott.

"Randall," she said, "this is Dr. Gladstone."

"Hello, Elena. What can I do for you? You need a
couple of mill?"

"Thanks but no thanks. It's time for your
checkup. I've managed to squirrel an hour away right
after lunch."

"Sorry. I can't make it. My schedule's full up."

"Mr. Lippincott told me to call you," she said.
"You know how he is."

Randall Lippincott sighed. "He makes me crazy
with all this nonsense," he said. "Checkups, vitamin

shots, tests. Why can't I be a normal walking wreck just like everybody else?"

"I'm sorry, dear," said Dr. Gladstone. "You'll have to take that up with him. One o'clock?"

"I'll be there."

CHAPTER SIX

Ruby Gonzalez choked back her disgust as she looked down filth-littered East Seventh Street. Zack Meadows's last address was in a fourth-floor walkup, a half-block east of the Bowery, a street so sodden and degenerate that it had lent its once-proud Dutch name to a way of life, as in "Bowery bum."

She walked down the block toward Meadows's building, which was jammed neatly in between a store that sold handmade leather purses and belts and had gone out of business, apparently failing to realize that the belts that were important in the Bowery weren't made of leather, and a cheese store, which did better than the belt shop because it also sold wine.

The litter in front of Meadows's building was so thick and resolute, it looked as if it had been brewed and boiled to a uniform consistency and then spray-painted on the sidewalk.

In this section of town, the news from uptown about people being required to clean up after their dogs hadn't yet arrived, because the sidewalk and the gutter and the street were festooned with dog reminders.

Ruby picked her way neatly through the piles and

walked up the cracked concrete steps of the building. She had been in New York often enough to know that doorbells in places like this never worked, so she looked for the superintendent's apartment number, which was written on the wall with a magic marker, then slipped the inside lock with a credit card from a Wisconsin cheese-by-mail shop.

The sign outside the apartment door said "Mr. Armaducci." Ruby rang the superintendent's bell. She had been prepared to charm the super when he appeared, but a look at the hulk wearing a strapped undershirt with hair on the tops of his shoulders was too much, even for Ruby's well-defined sense of duty.

He growled at her, "Wotcha want?" and she fished in her pocketbook and came up with a laminated card that identified her as a member of the Federal Bureau of Investigation.

He fingered the card with grease-stained fingers and she made a mental note to throw it away as soon as she got back outside.

"I want to see the Meadows apartment," she said.

"Yeah?" he said in the clever patois that all New Yorkers learn, as a consequence of their school system being the most expensive to operate in the United States.

"Gee, you got it. First time too," Ruby said.

"You got a warrant?" Mr. Armaducci said. That was the second thing New Yorkers learned to say. It gave them their world-wide reputation for sophistication.

"Do I need one?" Ruby asked.

"You got no warrant, you don't get to see nuthin'."

"If I have to go get a warrant, I won't come back alone," Ruby said.

"No?"

"I'll bring back half the health department," she said.

"Big deal. Wha they gonna do, fine the landlord? How the hell they fine him, I can't even find him."

"Fine the landlord, hell," Ruby said. "They take one look at this dump and they'll drag you out into the street and shoot you. Bang, bang."

"Very funny."

"Keys to the Meadows apartment."

"You wait here. I see I find dem."

It took five minutes for Mr. Armaducci to find the keys. From the looks of them, it was apparent that he had been keeping them hidden in a pot of boiling chicken grease on his stove.

"You see dat Meadows," the superintendent said, "you tell him I tron him out, he tree weeks behind da rent."

"And places like this aren't easy to find, either," Ruby said.

"Dat's right," the superintendent said. He scratched that sixty percent of his stomach that did not fit beneath his undershirt and he belched. Ruby walked away before he relieved himself in the hall which, judging from the smell, seemed to be the habit of the building's occupants.

"Which is his?" she asked.

"Tade flaw leff," the superintendent said.

As she walked up the creaking steps, Ruby wondered if there were perhaps a special subspecies of human who became New York City apartment superintendents. Surely, the preponderance among them of Mr. Armaduccis could not be explained away by the laws of probability.

Not the building or the hallway or the superintendent had prepared Ruby for the inside of Zack Meadows's apartment. It looked as if it had been used for the last ten years as a staging area for an army laundry. Clothes, all of them dirty, littered every corner of the two small rooms. The sink was filled with a lifetime supply of plastic plates and styrofoam cups. She sighed and thought to herself that white folks sure lived funny.

But the apartment would be easy to search. She merely had to drag her feet to turn over all the junk that was on the floor and the only two places where anything of value might have been hidden were a green enamel bedroom dresser and in a drawer under the sink. Ruby did not exactly know what she was looking for but there was nothing in either place that told anything about Zack Meadows except that he was a slob who didn't own any clean clothes.

Ruby spent an hour kicking about the apartment, but she found nothing. No phone numbers on the inside of the three-year-old telephone book, no addresses of friends or relatives. Just one old penny arcade photograph, presumably of Zack Meadows. She thought he looked stupid. She found a pile of old racing forms and skimmed them quickly. She noticed large x's drawn through the past performance charts of certain horses, as if they had automatically been eliminated from contention. All the horses so treated had jockeys with Italian-sounding names.

Ruby was sure she had found her man.

Finally, with a deep feeling of disgust, she turned

over the once-white plastic garbage pail. Stuffed into the bottom of it, along with a few small paper bags, were a fistful of napkins printed in bleeding red ink "Manny's Sandwich Shop." It gave an address around the corner on the Bowery.

Ruby locked the door behind her and stopped at Mr. Armaducci's apartment to return the keys.

"Did Meadows ever have any visitors?" she asked.

"Naaah, nobody come to see him."

"Thanks." She gave him the keys, avoiding skin contact with his hand.

"Hey," he called after her.

Ruby turned.

"You didden take nuttin' witcha, didja?"

"God, I hope not," Ruby said.

Manny's Sandwich Shop around the corner was just what the neighborhood deserved and Manny, the owner, seemed to have spent his life trying to live up to the quality of the restaurant.

He knew Zack Meadows well.

"Sure," Manny told Ruby. "He stops in here, two, three times a week. Likes my pastrami sandwiches."

"I bet they're wonderful," Ruby said. "I'm looking for him. You seen him around recently?"

Manny shrugged. "Let me think. No, maybe a couple weeks I ain't seen him."

"You have any idea where he hangs out?" Ruby asked. "Who his friends might be?"

Manny shook his head. "I never seen him with nobody. What you wanna know for?" he asked suspiciously.

Ruby winked. "My boss sent me down. I've got some money for him."

"Money? For Meadows?" Manny wrinkled his nose in disbelief.

"Yeah," Ruby said.

"Who's your boss?"

"You'd know him if I said it," Ruby said. "Meadows did some work on the big man's wife, if you know what I mean." She looked at him with a wise face that Manny searched for a few moments before nodding.

"Sometimes he used to hang out at the Bowery Bar," Manny said. "Maybe they seen him. Ernie there used to take Meadows's action," which meant, Ruby knew, that Ernie was the detective's bookie.

Ernie was sitting inside the door of the bar. He wore a blue pin-striped suit, had pink-tinted eyeglasses, and a pinkie ring with a tiger's eye stone that looked like a dinosaur egg with a crack in it. He kept looking over his shoulder at the street outside.

He made a pass at Ruby, seemed relieved when she sloughed it off, and then seemed happy to talk about Zack Meadows.

"A good dear friend," Ernie said. "You can tell him that and tell him to come and visit me. He ain't got nothing to be afraid of."

"I'm looking for him too," Ruby said.

"He owe you money too?" asked Ernie.

"No, but I've got some money for him."

Ernie looked up from his beer glass filled with red wine. "Yeah?" He seemed suddenly interested. "How much?"

"I don't actually have it on me. But it's five hundred dollars," Ruby said. "I've got to bring him to my boss to get it."

"Five hundred, huh? That's enough."

"Enough for what?"

"For him to pay up."

"So you got any idea where I can find him?" Ruby asked.

"If I knew, I woulda found him myself," said Ernie.

"You know anybody who was his friend?"

"Naaah, he got no friends." Ernie sipped his wine. "Wait a minute. Up on Twenty-second Street, there's . . ." He paused. "You find him, you see that I get three hundred out of that five hundred?"

"You got it," Ruby said. "When I find him, I'll take him to my boss for the money, then I'll personally drive him back here."

"All right. I guess I gotta trust you. There's this broad named Flossie. She hangs out on Twenty-second between Eighth and Ninth. In the saloons there. She used to be a hooker. Maybe she still is. Meadows hangs around with her. I think he lives with her sometimes."

"Flossie?"

"Yeah. You see her, you know her. She's like five hundred pounds. Watch out she don't sit on you."

"Thanks, Ernie," Ruby said. "When I find him, I'll bring him back here."

When Ruby went outside, a New York City tow truck operator was attaching a chain to the bumper of her white Lincoln Continental.

"Hey, hold on," she yelled. "That's my car."

The driver was a fat black man with a slicked-down hairdo that made him look like a 1930s opening act at the Cotton Club.

"Illegally parked, honey," he said.

"How? Where?" Ruby said. "Where's the sign?"

"Down there." The driver pointed vaguely down the block. When Ruby strained her eyes, she was able to see some sort of sign on a utility pole.

"What's that sign got to do with up here?" she said.

"I ain't in charge of signs," the driver said. "I just tow away the cars."

"What's this gonna cost me?" she asked.

"Seventy five dollars. Twenty five for the ticket. Fifty for the tow."

"Let's try coexisting," Ruby said. "I'll give you fifty now, and you let the car down."

The driver winked at her. "You give me eighty now and I'll let you down."

"You know," Ruby said, "it ain't just that you're a turkey, you be greedy too."

"Ninety," the driver said.

"And you're ugly, to boot," Ruby said.

"Up to a hundred," the driver said. He bent under Ruby's bumper to fasten the chain.

Ruby walked to the front of the tow truck. She let the air out of the front left tire, then out of the right front tire. The heavy truck settled down onto its rims.

The driver heard the hiss and came to the front of his truck, just as a cab was stopping to pick up Ruby.

"Hey, you," the driver called. "What'm I gonna do now?"

"Call a tow truck," Ruby said. "And then when I got your ass in front of the license board next week, you better call youself a lawyer." She looked to the cab driver. "Twenty-second Street," she said.

CHAPTER SEVEN

Randall Lippincott was whistling when he got back to his office at 2:15 P.M., an act so abnormal that his two secretaries looked at each other in disbelief.

"The next thing you know, he'll do a dance on the desk," one of the secretaries said.

"Yeah, and I'll be elected the new Pope," said Janie, the senior of the two secretaries by six months.

Being elected Pope might not have been as big a surprise for Janie as what happened when she answered the buzzer and walked into Lippincott's office at 2:30.

The banker had loosened his tie and opened his shirt collar. He was still whistling.

"Are you all right, sir?" she asked.

"Never better. Feel like a new man," he said. "Send out and get me a bottle of beer, will you? That's a good girl."

At 2:50, Lippincott was not so sure that he was feeling all that well. He took off his jacket and his tie. At 2:55, his shirt went and when Janie came back in with the beer, he was sitting behind his desk in a tee shirt. She almost dropped the beer when she saw him.

He ignored her surprise and stood up to kick off his shoes. "I hate clothes," he said. "Just hate them. That my beer? Good."

He drank from the can, then put it on the desk, and peeled off his tee shirt.

The secretary noticed that his skin was pale with reddish blotches, the kind of skin she would have expected an out-of-shape, overweight, forty-five-year-old to have.

She stood fascinated, watching, unmoving, but when Lippincott opened his belt and began to unzip his trouser fly, she turned and walked quickly from the office.

At her desk, she consulted her appointment book and had a problem. A vice president of Chase Manhattan bank was due for a meeting at 3:15. How could she make sure that her boss was wearing clothes for the meeting?

She thought about it until 3:10, then took a deep breath, summoned up her courage and walked back into his office. She stopped in disbelief inside the door. Lippincott was lying on the couch, naked, squirming as if the smooth polished fabric of the sofa irritated his skin.

He saw her in the doorway.

"Hi," he said with a wave. "Come on in."

She stood resolutely still, averting her eyes. "Mr. Lippincott, you've got a meeting with Chase Manhattan in five minutes."

"Good. I'm here."

"Err, I don't think you can hold that meeting without clothes, Mr. Lippincott."

He looked down at his naked body as if noticing it for the first time. "Suppose you're right," he said.

"God, I hate clothes. Maybe I could wear a sheet. Tell them I just came from a toga party. Think that'll work? Can you find me a sheet?"

He looked at her hopefully. She shook her head no. He sighed in resignation.

"No, I suppose you're right. Okay. I'll get dressed."

When the man from Chase Manhattan arrived a few minutes later, she called Lippincott from the outside office and asked him pointedly, "Are you ready for the meeting, sir?"

"Of course," he said. "Oh. Oh. I see. You mean, do I have my clothes on? Sure, I do. Send him in."

The secretary escorted the guest inside.

Lippincott was sitting behind his desk. He was in his shirt sleeves and not wearing a tie. Normally over-polite, this time Lippincott did not rise to greet his guest, but merely waved him to a chair. With a sinking horror, Janie glanced over to a corner of the office. On the floor there, she saw Lippincott's jacket and tie, his tee shirt and undershorts, his shoes and socks. He was sitting behind his desk wearing only shirt and trousers. In bare feet. She wanted to scream.

"Will there be anything else, sir?" she forced herself to ask.

"No, no, Janie. Everything's okay," Lippincott said. As she left the office, he called after her, "Don't go home without talking to me first," he said.

The meeting lasted for two hours, because there was a shopping list of business to be concluded between the two banking empires. The man from Chase Manhattan knew he had to ignore the way the usually-impeccable Lippincott was dressed and remind himself he was in a cage with a financial tiger.

But he soon realized that on this day Lippincott was a toothless tiger. He seemed agreeable to anything Chase Manhattan wanted.

"Would you steer me wrong?" he kept asking, with an insouciant smile and the man, who would steer his mother into crystal radio stocks, was forced to shake his head. "No, no. Not me." It was like taking candy from a baby.

Randall Lippincott kept checking his watch, which he had taken off and placed in front of him on his brown desk blotter. He rubbed his bare wrist as if the feeling of the watch pained him.

The man from Chase Manhattan left.

In the outer office, Janie Wanamaker had been sitting quietly since 4:30, ready to leave. The other secretary had already gone for the night with a look of compassionate condolence at the one who had to stay. Janie fixed her lipstick for the fourth time and her eye shadow for the third.

It wasn't like Randall Lippincott to work late or to ask his secretary to work late. In fact, he was so undemanding on his secretaries that Janie had thought she had been hired for her bustline or her long legs, but when six months had gone by without Lippincott's making a pass at her, she decided she was wrong.

As the man from Chase Manhattan left, he told Janie: "Mr. Lippincott wants to see you now."

She went inside fearing the worst. Perhaps he had stripped naked again. There was his brother's suicide in Tokyo. Maybe the Lippincotts had a streak of family insanity running through all of them that manifested itself all at once in midlife.

But Lippincott was still sitting behind his desk in his shirt sleeves.

He smiled at Janie when she came in and the smile was so broad that she tilted a little more toward the insanity theory.

"Janie," Lippincott said, then paused. "I don't quite know how to say this."

Janie didn't quite know how to respond so she waited silently for Lippincott to continue.

"Errr," he said, "are you doing anything tonight? Before you say anything, I just want you to know that I'm not making a pass or anything but I just feel like going out and I'd like somebody to go out with."

He looked at her hopefully.

"Well, I . . ."

"Anyplace you'd like to go," he said. "Dinner. Dancing. Disco duck dancing, is that what they call it? That's where I'd like to go."

The truth was that Janie Wanamaker had no date that night and an evening out with Randall Lippincott didn't sound half bad.

"Well, I . . ." she started again.

"Good," he said. "What place would you like to go?"

She thought immediately of the latest New York in disco, a place whose management was so rude that its attraction for New Yorkers was total. Each night, the disco attracted hundreds more people than it could hold, but there were some reservations that they had to honor. Randall Lippincott was one.

"I'll go out to my desk and make reservations," Janie said. "Meanwhile, perhaps you can get your clothes on?" she asked hopefully.

She telephoned and felt the exhilarating glow of

power as she made reservations for Randall Lippin-cott and Miss Janie Wanamaker. Six times she had stood outside that same disco on cold nights hoping to be chosen for admittance and six times she had been ignored. Tonight would be different. Tonight was her turn to be haughty and patronizing.

She waited in her office. Lippincott came out five minutes later, fully-dressed but with his tie still loose around his neck and looking uncomfortable, wearing his shirt and jacket again.

They ate dinner at a restaurant near the bank and Lippincott itched all through the meal, even as he told her of his ambition to go to a South Seas island and live like a native, walking the beaches and eating clams.

"A life-long dream?" Janie asked.

"No. Actually, it just came on me this afternoon," Lippincott said. "But some things are so right that you don't bother to question them, no matter when they come."

She was glad he hadn't asked her to feed him at her apartment. Like all single New York women, her apartment was a mess and to get it ready for a dinner guest she would have had to take ten days off from her job.

They lingered a long time over drinks. Randall Lippincott, she decided, was a nice and gentle man and she had the feeling that if it had not been for the backing of the rest of his family, he was too soft a man to have become a multi-millionaire on his own. His character, like his face and body, seemed to have no bone in it, no central core of hardness that Janie felt acquiring riches required.

But she found him charming in a silly kind of way.

He talked about the small pleasures of life, walking on the sand, swimming naked on a private beach near Hawaii, running through the woods after his prize pair of Gordon Setters, looking at planets through a high-powered telescope. The high point of his life seemed to have been riding over the Los Angeles Coliseum in the Goodyear Blimp.

After many drinks and four cups of coffee, they were ready to leave and Lippincott seemed calmly looking forward to the evening. Despite the disparity in their ages, Janie began to wonder if perhaps Randall Lippincott was on the verge of busting up his marriage, and suppose he were, and even though she was just his secretary, who knew what could happen? Stranger things had happened. She resolved that if he wanted to spend the night at her apartment, she would allow it. She would make him wait in the hallway for ten minutes under some sort of pretext, while she raced around inside putting the piles into piles.

It was after nine o'clock when they got to the disco. Lippincott had taken his tie off in the cab and gave it to the driver. Already a crowd of twenty persons stood around outside the building, hoping that tonight they would be among the anointed ones allowed in.

Janie led Lippincott from the taxicab to the man guarding the door. His look was surly, the kind of look favored by the incompetent given power over the inconsequential.

"Mr. Lippincott and Miss Wanamaker," said Janie officiously. The door guard looked past her, saw and recognized Lippincott, and his face changed into an unaccustomed smile.

"Of course," he said. "Go right in."

Janie smiled and took Lippincott's arm. Who knows, she thought. Millionaires had married their secretaries before. Who was to say it couldn't happen again?

Inside, the lights were pulsating in time with the incessant 120 beats a minute of the recorded music. Couples crowded the small dance floor. They wore sequins, see-through plastic, opaque plastic, leather, furs, and feathers.

Lippincott looked around in surprise. "So this is what it's like," he said.

Janie felt a sense of satisfaction as she took his hand and was able to say "Yes. It's this way all the time."

They followed a waiter to a table and gave him an order for drinks.

Lippincott was thumping his hands heavily on the small round table. Suddenly he stood and took off his jacket. He sat back down in shirt sleeves. Janie didn't mind at all, even though if some other escort had done it, she would have been mortified. No one was about to tell Randall Lippincott to leave because he wasn't dressed right.

She looked around the place while Lippincott, with a spoon, happily banged out the rhythm on the side of a water glass. She saw two movie stars, a famous rock singer, and a well-known literary figure who had given up writing for talking on television shows.

Her night was made. She would have talking rights on this evening with her friends for years to come.

"Can't stand these clothes," Lippincott said. "Come on, want to dance?"

"Do you know how?" Janie asked. It would be

awful to be embarrassed in front of all these people. Then she had another thought. How could someone be embarrassed by dancing with Randall Lippincott? No matter how badly he danced?

"No, but it looks easy," Lippincott said. He reached out for her hand and led her to the floor, just as the waiter arrived with their drinks.

On the floor, Janie slipped easily into the hip-swaying solo steps of her dance. Randall Lippincott was just as bad as she thought he would be. Perhaps even worse. He lumbered about the floor, waving his arms inconsequentially, and not even making a pretense of stomping in time to the music.

But he was laughing aloud, having a good time, and seemed uncaring of the eyes watching him. Every time he saw someone doing a step or a routine he liked, he tried it, and after only a few moments, Janie stopped being self-conscious about dancing with him and laughingly joined in his spirit of good fun.

Perhaps it was the first time in his life that Randall Lippincott had ever laughed, she thought. Really laughed.

It was certainly the last.

Three minutes into the dance, puffing and laughing, Lippincott had unbuttoned his shirt and tossed it onto an empty chair.

His tee shirt followed a minute later and then, as if the dam of inhibitions had finally surrendered, he sat on the floor to take off his trousers, his shoes and his socks. People by now had stopped to watch. Waiters were hovering at the edge of the floor, helplessly wondering what to do.

He tossed all his clothes toward a chair. Most of them landed on the floor.

"Please, Mr. Lippincott," Janie said.

But he did not hear her. His eyes were closed as he galumphed up and down, back and forth, wearing only his boxer shorts, and then, as the record played of a disco singer doing the only hit song ever written about a cake in the rain, he hooked his thumbs into the elastic waistband of his shorts and shimmied them off.

Janie Wanamaker was horrified. It took another full minute for the staff to realize they should do something, and just as they came up to wrap a table cloth around Randall Lippincott's naked body, all the happy intensity seemed to ooze from him and he sat down on the floor shivering, trying to squirm out from under the table cloth, and crying.

Large tears.

CHAPTER EIGHT

In the private East Side clinic to which Randall Lippincott had been taken, his doctor patted the man gently on the arm. Lippincott was lying in a bed, his arms locked down by restraint cuffs.

"How's my little naked disco dancer?" the doctor asked.

Lippincott was calm now and he looked up hopefully at his doctor who said, "Don't worry about a thing, Randall. Everything's going to be all right."

The doctor searched through a medical bag for a few moments, withdrawing a syringe and a vial of yellow liquid. The syringe was quickly filled and the doctor inserted it into the vein inside Lippincott's left elbow.

He winced at the small pinch of pain. The doctor withdrew the needle, and even though it was a disposable syringe, dropped it back into the medical bag.

The doctor patted his forehead.

"Everything's going to be all right," she said, then Dr. Elena Gladstone snapped shut her medical bag and walked to the door. Lippincott's worried eyes followed her.

At the door, she turned and said, "Goodbye, Randall. And I do mean goodbye."

She smiled for a moment. Lippincott's eyes showed his confusion and fright. Then she laughed aloud, throwing her head back and tossing her long red hair, before she walked from the room.

In the hallway, she glanced to her right. Standing in front of the nurse's desk, their backs to her, she saw the young white man and the old Oriental she had seen that morning at Elmer Lippincott's estate. She quickly walked across the hall and disappeared through an exit door.

She walked down two flights of stairs, and then into another patient area of the clinic. In the patient lounge, she found a pay phone and placed a thirty-five-cent call.

When the phone was answered, she said:

"This is Elena. He'll be gone in five minutes."

Then she hung up.

The nurse had never had anybody as important as a Lippincott on her floor before. On the other hand, no one had ever looked into her eyes like the thin dark-haired man who stood smiling in front of her. His eyes were deep pools of darkness, and they seemed to act like vacuums, sucking her emotion out of her, through her eyes, and she pointed down the hall toward Lippincott's room.

"Room twenty-two-twelve," she said.

"Thanks," Remo said. "I'll remember this."

"You're coming back, aren't you?" the nurse asked.

"Nothing would keep me away," Remo said. Chiun smirked.

92

"When?" the nurse asked. "You coming right back?

"Well, I've got a couple of things to do first," Remo said, "but then I'll be back. You can count on it."

"I work till 12:30. I get off then," the nurse said. "I don't live alone but my roommate's a stewardess for Pan-Am and she's in Guam or someplace like that. There's nobody at my place. Except me. And whoever I bring."

"Sounds good to me," Remo said. He took Chiun's arm and led him down the hall.

"This country is exceeding strange," Chiun said.

"Why?" Remo asked.

"The adoration from that girl. Why, with all the people in this country, most of them better looking than you and all of them smarter than you, why does she choose you to fall in love with?"

"Must be my native charm," Remo said.

"I would have suggested brain damage," Chiun said.

"You're jealous," Remo said. "That's all. The green-eyed monster has got you."

"One does not overly concern oneself with the doings of nincompoops," Chiun said.

Inside Room 2212, Randall Lippincott had the sheet inside his mouth. He was trying to bite his way through it.

Remo came to his bedside and took the sheet out of his mouth.

"You don't know us," he said, "but we work for your father. What happened tonight?"

"Sheets," Lippincott hissed. "Got to get them off me. Suffocating. Too much clothes." His eyes were

93

wild and flashing from side to side, blinking rapidly.

Remo looked to Chiun and the tiny Oriental moved quickly to the bed and released Lippincott's wrist restraints. The man's hands, once freed, pulled the sheet from his body and then began to claw at the neck of his long hospital gown.

The gown separated as his pale white hands pulled off the buttons and he yanked the gown from his shoulders and lay naked on the bed. He looked around him, eyes darting feverishly, a cornered rat looking for an escape route.

"Heavy," he hissed. "Heavy."

"You are all right now," Chiun said. "Nothing will harm you." To Remo, he said softly, "He is most seriously ill."

"Heavy, heavy," Lippincott said again. "The air. Coming down. Crushing me." He began to flail his arms in the air above his head.

"What's going on, Chiun?" asked Remo, feeling helpless as he stood at the foot of the bed, watching the sick man.

"Some evil medicine has been worked on him," Chiun said. "Very evil."

Lippincott waved his arms as if trying to swipe his way through a cloud of summer gnats. Saliva dribbled down the side of his mouth. His pasty face turned blotchy, then began to grow deep red.

"What do we do?" asked Remo.

Chiun touched the fingertips of his right hand to Lippincott's solar plexus. He probed for a moment. Lippincott ignored him, as if he did not know there was anyone else in the room.

Chiun nodded to himself, then grabbed Lippincott's left wrist. The flailing arm stopped as if it had

94

abruptly punched into a pool of tar. Chiun looked at the inside joint of the elbow, then nodded toward Remo, who leaned over and saw the small pinprick of a hypodermic in the joint of the elbow.

Chiun released Lippincott's hand, which began swinging about his head again. His wispy white hair fluttering about his head, Chiun moved quickly. He touched a finger into the left side of Lippincott's throat. The arms continued to flail, the eyes to roll, the saliva to flow, but then the arms began to slow down and the eyes began to steady.

Chiun pressed for a few seconds more and Lippincott's eyes closed. His arms dropped heavily onto the bed.

"There is a poison in his body," Chiun said, "and it attacks his brain. All his motions have helped to pump that poison into his brain."

"Can we do anything?"

Chiun moved around to the other side of the bed.

"We must close off the brain so no more poison gets in. Then we can hope that his body can cleanse itself of the evil."

He pressed his fingers into the right side of Lippincott's throat. The man was already asleep, but slowly the red color began to drain from his face.

Chiun held the pressure for exactly ten seconds, then leaned across Lippincott's body to thrust his fingers into the millionaire's left armpit.

Chiun hissed under his breath. Remo recognized the Korean word for "live." Chiun pronounced it as an order.

Remo nodded as he saw that Chiun was closing off, one by one, the major blood vessels in Lippincott's body. It was an old Sinanju technique to pre-

95

vent poison from coursing freely through a victim's body. When Chiun had first explained it to Remo, Remo had called it a "touch tourniquet," and Chiun, surprised that Remo had actually understood something, had nodded and smiled. The pressure applications had to be done precisely, and in exact order, so that the major blood vessels that carried the poison were sealed off temporarily, but the auxiliary blood vessels still carried enough fresh blood and oxygen to the brain to keep it alive. In a surgical amphitheater, the procedure would have taken six medical specialists, a dozen technicians, and a million dollars worth of equipment. Chiun did it with his fingertips.

Remo had never learned the sequence but now as he watched Chiun work over Lippincott from throat to ankle, he saw for the first time the specific logic of it. Left side, right side, left side, right side, top to bottom. Sixteen points that had to be hit. And one error could cause almost instant death from oxygen starvation of the brain.

Without thinking, he said, "Be careful, Chiun."

The Oriental turned his hazel eyes on Remo, staring at him with disdain, while digging his fingers deep into Lippincott's left thigh muscle.

"Careful?" he hissed. "If you had learned this when it was offered you, it would be done twice as quickly and he would have more chance to live. If it goes wrong, do not blame me," he said. "I know how to do it. Because I have bothered to learn. It is just that I can never rely upon cheap white help for anything."

"Right, right, right, right," said Remo. "Stay with it, Chiun."

To keep himself busy, Remo went to the front of

the bed and began to monitor Lippincott's pulse. As he stood alongside the man, a flowery smell insinuated itself into his senses. It was a smell he had encountered before. Sweet and musky. He put it out of his mind, and with his hand on Lippincott's chest, monitored the heart rate and breathing rate simultaneously. When Chiun finished with the large vein in Lippincott's right ankle, the man's pulse was beating at only thirty beats a minute, his respiration rate was only one breath every sixteen seconds.

Chiun stopped and looked up. Remo lifted his hand from Lippincott's chest.

"Will he live?" Remo asked.

"If he does, I hope he never has to suffer the indignity of trying to teach something to some person who does not wish to learn, and who rejects the gift as if it were the footmud of a . . ."

"Will he live, Chiun?" Remo asked again.

"I do not know. The poison was much in his system. It depends on how much he wishes to live."

"You keep saying poison," Remo said. "What kind of poison?"

Chiun shook his head. "This is a thing I do not know, a poison that does not injure the body but changes the mind. This fighting one's clothing. This feeling that the air itself is a heavy blanket. These things I do not understand."

"It happened to his brother too," Remo said. "Afraid of Japanese."

Chiun looked at Remo quizzically.

"We are talking about poison of the brain. What does that have to do with it?"

"His brother. He couldn't stand being in a room with Japanese," Remo said.

"That is not mind poison," Chiun said. "That is just good taste. Can you not tell the difference?"

"Please, Chiun, no lectures about the pushy Japanese. Anyway, this guy's brother dove out a window because he couldn't stand them."

"How high a window?" Chiun asked.

"Six stories."

"And the doors to this room were not nailed shut?" Chiun asked.

"No."

"Well, perhaps that was a little extreme," Chiun said. "Six stories." He thought about it for a moment. "Yes, that was extreme. About three stories extreme," he said. "No one should ever jump out a window more than three stories high to avoid the Japanese, if the windows and doors are not bolted and nailed shut."

Remo watched Lippincott carefully. A sense of peace seemed to have overtaken his body. The tenseness that had bunched up his shoulders and hips was slowly passing from his body, which was softening into a relaxed and deep sleep.

"I think he's going to be all right, Chiun," Remo offered.

"Silence," thundered Chiun. "What do you know?" He touched Lippincott's throat, and then the pit of his stomach, probing deeply with the balls of his fingers.

"He is going to be all right," Chiun said.

"I wonder if that injection in the arm had anything to do with this," Remo said.

Chiun shrugged. "I do not understand your western medicine, ever since I stopped watching Rad Rex

98

as Dr. Bruce Barton, when the show became vile and obscene. Since then, nothing is the same."

"I wonder who his doctor was," Remo said. He went back to the nurse's station, but the nurse only knew that every doctor in the hospital had looked in on Lippincott. She had a list of names a full page long.

Remo nodded and began to walk away.

"When will I see you?" the nurse asked.

"Very soon," Remo said with a smile.

Lippincott was stiill sleeping when Remo returned and Chiun was watching him, a pleased and self-satisfied look on his face. Remo used the telephone in the room to dial a number that reported on the winning lottery numbers in the 463 separate lotteries held in the New York-New Jersey-Connecticut area. To get all the numbers, a person at a pay phone had to drop nine dimes into the coin box. Remo listened as the tape recorded voice began to spin out the winning combinations of numbers, and Remo said deliberately: "Blue and Gold. Silver and Gray," and then gave the number he read on the base of Lippincott's telephone.

He hung up and within a minute, the telephone rang.

"Smitty?" Remo said as he lifted the receiver.

"Yes, what is it?"

"Randall Lippincott's in the hospital. He went some kind of crazy. I think it might be like his brother."

"Yes, I know," said Smith. "How is he?"

"Chiun says he'll live. But he needs a guard here. Can you get somebody from the family or something?"

"Yes," Smith said. "I'll have somebody there soon."

"We'll wait for him. Another thing. Check what you've got on the Lippincotts. There was a doctor here who might have shot Randall up with something to kill him. See if you can find any link among the Lippincotts. Same doctor or something." The smell of flowers was again strong in Remo's nose.

"All right," Smith said.

"Anything from Ruby yet?" Remo asked.

"Not a word."

"Hah. So much for women," said Remo.

CHAPTER NINE

Elena Gladstone was asleep in the third floor bedroom of the brownstone on East Eighty-first Street. She slept naked and when the private telephone rang, she sat up in bed and cradled the telephone against her shoulder. The sheet slid from her body.

"This is Dr. Gladstone," she said. She listened as she heard a familiar voice, then sat straight up in bed, away from the headboard, as if startled.

"Alive?" she said. "He can't be. I administered the shot myself."

She listened again. "I saw them there but they couldn't . . ."

"I don't know," she said. "I'll have to think about it. They are still at the clinic?"

She paused and pondered. "I'll talk to you tomorrow," she said.

After she replaced the telephone, she remained sitting up in bed. She could not understand how the old Oriental and the young white man had saved Randall Lippincott's life. It wasn't possible, not with the shot she had given him. But they had done it, and even now guards were on their way to protect Lippincott. If he recovered, he would be sure to talk.

Something would have to be done about him. And

about the two intruders, because she still had more Lippincotts to kill.

She thought of the two. The Oriental. The young American. And as she thought of Remo and his deep eyes and the smile that bared his teeth and moved his lips but never extended to his eyes, she shuddered involuntarily and pulled the sheet up around her body.

They had to go. In the case of the American, it was a shame, but she could do it.

She reached for the telephone.

Ruby Gonzalez had hit every saloon on Twenty-second Street searching for Flossie. She hadn't realized that white folks had so many saloons, that white saloons had so many drunks and that so many drunks thought they were God's gift to young unescorted black women. Not that any of them throught so much about it that they would buy her a drink. She had bought her own in the first six saloons, a vile concoction of orange juice and wine. She had been raised on it as orange juice and champagne but there was no champagne to be found in these Twenty-second Street saloons.

She had started out by hanging out in the taverns, hoping to get someone in conversation and find out about Flossie, but that hadn't worked, and so, after six bars and twelve OJ and wines, she had stopped drinking and stopped hanging out. Instead, she walked into the bar, accosted the bartender and asked if he knew where she could find Flossie.

Bartender: "Who wants to know?"
Ruby: "You know who she is?"
Bartender: "No."

Ruby: "Big fat woman. Blonde."

Bartender: "Why you want her?"

Ruby: "You know her?"

Bartender: "No. What do you want her for?"

Ruby: "She's my nanny, sucker, and I come to take her back home to Tara."

Bartender: "Oh, yeah?"

Next bar.

And now she was down to the last bar on Twenty-second Street, as far west as one could go without falling into the Hudson River. Or, more accurately, onto it because the river debris was so thick, the water had the consistency of limestone. If the river were any dirtier, you could ice skate on it in July.

She walked into the final bar.

Pay dirt.

At the end of the bar, she saw a blonde woman partially sitting on the stool.

The woman overflowed the stool, her giant buttocks surrounding it, covering the top and hiding it from view. She wore a red and blue flowered dress. Her upper arms were massive and her hair a tangled mass of every-which-way strings. Ruby thought that if it hadn't been for the fat and the dirt and the ugly dress and the uncombed hair and the bleary blue eyes and the double and triple chins and the arms that were shaped like legs of lamb, big legs of lamb, Flossie would still have been homely. Her nose was too broad and her mouth too small and her eyes were set too close together in her head. Even at her best, she would have been pretty bad, Ruby decided.

Ruby ignored the surprised look of the bartender and the greetings of four bums sitting at the bar and walked toward the back and sat on the stool next to Flossie.

The fat woman turned to stare at her. Ruby Gonzalez smiled, that quick sudden smile that could melt people's hearts and turn stranger into life-long friend.

"Hi, Flossie," she said. "Have a drink?" Ruby nodded toward the empty beer glass and took a five dollar bill from her jacket pocket where she kept saloon money. It invited trouble to open a purse and fish in a wallet for cash in places like this. Too many people watched and wondered.

Flossie nodded. "Sure," she said. "Roger," she called. "A drink for me and my friend." She turned back to Ruby. "Do I know you?" she asked thickly. "I don't think so 'cause I don't have too many friends of the black persuasion."

Her voice was slurred and she spoke slowly, as if trying to make sure that she said nothing wrong, nothing offensive, at least until the beer was bought and paid for.

"Sure," Ruby said. "I met you once with Zack."

"Zack? Zack? Oh, yeah. Zack. No, you didn't. I never met you with Zack. Zack doesn't like Negroes."

"I know," Ruby said. "He and I, well, we were never friends but we worked together on a case once."

The bartender appeared. Ruby ordered two beers. Flossie was still shaking her head. "Never saw you," she said. "Woulda remembered. Remember everybody as skinny as I used to be."

"I'll tell you when it was," Ruby said. "It was one night, maybe three, four months ago. I bumped into Zack down near Seventh Street where he lives, and we rode up to Twenty-third Street on the subway, and he said he was going to see you and we walked over near your place, and he met you downstairs, and we just waved at each other. I think you were going to get something to eat."

"Not Zack," Flossie said. "Zack never buys a meal."

"Maybe you were buying," Ruby said.

"Probably," Flossie agreed. "Give a man everything, best years of your life and have to feed him too."

"How is Zack anyway?" Ruby said. "Seen him lately?"

"Don't want to talk about it," Flossie said.

"Oh? Why not? What's he gone and done now?"

Flossie screwed up her face in intense concentration as if she were trying to recollect not only what Zack had done but exactly who he was.

"Oh, yeah," she said finally. "He left. He just walks out one night and doesn't come back. Leaves me without nothing to drink or eat. Leaves me alone. Had to go out on the street again to get something to drink and eat."

"When was that?" asked Ruby. The beers came and she hoisted her glass, clinked with Flossie's and toasted her impending good luck. "When was that?"

Flossie drained half the glass at a sip. "I don't know. Not too good on time."

"Two weeks ago?" Ruby said.

Flossie concentrated on the concept of weeks, then nodded. "Something like that, maybe. Or a month. I know a month. Thirty days has September, April, November, and June. All the rest have thirty-six except leap year which ends too soon." She finished her beer. "Something like that."

Ruby signalled for another beer for Flossie as she took a small sip of hers.

"Was he working on a big case?"

"Zack? Zack never had a big case in his life," Flossie said. "Trying to be the big man. Sitting there in my apartment, writing his dumb letter, messing it up, throwing papers on my floor. Is that any way to act? I ask you. Any way to act? Throwing papers on my clean floor. Dumb letter. Trying to be big man."

Her beer came and she concentrated on it.

"What'd he do with the letter?" Ruby asked.

Flossie shrugged, a small movement at the epicenter of her body that sent shock waves careening through the surrounding flesh for seconds after. Starting at her shoulders, the shrug shuddered downward until it reached the seat of the overburdened stool, and then the aftershocks caromed back up so that her shoulders, which started it all, shuddered again.

She drank her beer to calm the earthquake.

"What'd he do with the letter?" Ruby repeated.

"Who knows? Wrote it. Envelope. My stamp on it. My good stamp. Yeah. I mailed it."

"To the President?"

"Thass right. To the President of the United States of Watchamacallit, himself. I mailed it. Me. Zack can't even mail nothing right, I gotta mail it."

Ruby nodded. So much for the letter. Now the only question left was where was Zack Meadows.

Ruby drank with Flossie until the tavern closed, trying to get a clue on Meadows's whereabouts, but the big woman knew nothing.

Two barflies offered to walk them home but Flossie told them loudly that ladies like she and her friend Ruby did not have anything to do with lower-class people like that.

They laughed.

Ruby told them to fuck off.

Flossie led the way toward the door.

Ruby was following her.

One of the men staggered off his stool and grabbed Ruby's left arm.

Her right hand darted into her big oversized pocketbook and brought out a .32 caliber snubnose revolver, which she inserted into the man's left nostril.

His eyes widened in shock and he let go of Ruby's arm. He staggered back to his stool.

Ruby nodded wordlessly and replaced the gun. She met Flossie outside on the sidewalk.

"Gone home now," Flossie said.

"I'll walk with you," Ruby said.

"Don't has to walk with me. I walks all time myself."

"That's all right," Ruby said. "I'll walk with you anyway."

"Didden get chancet to clean apartment," Flossie said.

"All right," Ruby said. "Let's walk."

"Yeah. Walk," Flossie said.

The tenement building was the equivalent, in real property, of Flossie herself. It hadn't been much to start with and had decayed steadily. The halls were dark and Ruby regarded herself as lucky because at least she could not see the dirt.

Ruby went up the steps, placing her feet down delicately, ready to jump instantly if she should step down on something that squealed or moved. Flossie didn't seem to mind. She stomped up the steps like a Wagnerian soprano marching to center stage to sing about a horse.

Ruby reflected that the worst slums she had ever seen in the United States weren't black people's slums, they were white people's slums. Maybe for a white person to get as poor as a black person required some kind of extra effort, some special skill, the kind that could go into making a slum an absolute unliveable hovel.

"Ain't much," Flossie grunted halfway up to the third floor. "But all I can afford right now."

"Zack ever help you with the rent?" Ruby asked.

"He only helps racehorses with the rent. Bookies," Flossie said. She liked that so much she repeated it. "He only helps bookies with the rent."

Ruby had thought Zack Meadows's apartment was dirty, but compared with Flossie's, it looked like a Frank Lloyd Wright experiment in open, carefree living.

That the debris and clutter was neither new nor unusual, Flossie demonstrated by picking her way accurately through the piles of rubble, weaving her way to her bed, and collapsing on it in a landslide of moving flesh that rocked the bed.

"Good night, Flossie," Ruby said. "I'll see myself out."

The only answer was Flossie's raucous snoring. Ruby closed the door behind her and looked around the room. If Meadows had written his letter here, he would have done it at the kitchen table. Flossie had talked about his throwing papers on the floor. Ruby looked around under the table and against the wall, found three crumpled-up pieces of paper from a yellow legal-size pad.

She read them under the bare kitchen bulb. They represented Meadows's initial attempts to write his report to the President, before he had hit upon the unique literary device of attacking Italian jockeys and all policemen.

Ruby read the three pages and smiled to herself.

"Lifeline Laboratory," she said aloud. "Well, well, well, well, well."

She put the papers in her pocketbook, after first shaking them carefully to make sure there weren't carrying any nonpaying passengers, then let herself out of the apartment, locking it behind her.

Time to sleep. She would look into the Lifeline Laboratory tomorrow.

CHAPTER TEN

The two men had been following them since they had left the Upper East Side Clinic. Remo had known it without knowing why he knew it. He had not seen them and they had made no sound that any other pair of pedestrians would not have made, but they were not just pedestrians. They were following Chiun and him, and somehow he had just sensed their presence.

It was one of the problems of Sinanju, Remo thought. The discipline changed you, turned you into something else, but it did it without your conscious knowledge. Once, Smith had asked Remo how he had been able to do some special physical thing, and Remo could only tell him: "Because I can."

The question, Remo knew, was like asking an oak: "How did you become such a great tree?"

"I grew from a little acorn."

"But how?"

There was no answer to the how, no explanation, just as there was no explanation that Remo could give anyone about how he did what he did. Including to himself.

"Let's stop and look in this store window," Remo said to Chiun as they strolled down Sixtieth Street in

111

New York, near the south entrance to Central Park where horsedrawn hansom cabs were lined up, waiting for passengers. The cabs no longer rode their passengers through Central Park, preferring instead the relative safety of city streets. To ride through the park at night, they would have needed somebody next to the driver riding shotgun.

Chiun ignored Remo's suggestion and continued walking.

"I wanted to look in that store window," Remo said.

"It is not necessary," Chiun said. "There are two of them. Both large, blonde men, bigger than you. They are of the size of your football players and may be that because one of them walks with a slight limp. They are of the weight of seventeen stones. The one on the left moves nicely, smoothly. He is not the one who limps. The one who limps moves more with muscle than with grace."

"How do you know that?" Remo said, realizing he was asking Chiun the kind of question Smith occasionally asked Remo. How?

"How did you know they were following us?" Chiun asked back.

"I don't know. I just knew."

"As birds just fly? As fish just swim?" said Chiun.

"That's right," Remo said.

"Then you have no more sense than bird or fish," said Chiun, "because they have no choice but to fly and to swim, but you have learned to do what you do, and how can you learn something without knowing it?"

"I don't know, Little Father, and if you're going to

start yelling abuse at me, I don't want to talk about it."

Chiun shook his head. He jammed his hands even farther up into the sleeves of his green and yellow brocaded kimono. The kimono, at the bottom, ballooned out like a child's hoop skirt so that Chiun's slipper-clad feet were not visible, no matter how rapidly he walked.

"You were aware of them, Remo," said Chiun, "because as you live, you move through a field of force. It emanates from you and it surrounds you, and when other people or things move into that field, they disturb it and send some of that force back to you. That is how you knew they were there, because for thirteen of your blocks they have been moving within your field and finally even your dulled senses picked up their existence."

"All right," said Remo. "Then how come *I* don't know how big they are or that one limps or how they move?"

"Because you are like a child with a gun. He thinks that because he knows how to squeeze the trigger, he knows everything there is to know about marksmanship. It is a wise child who learns that he does not know everything and tries to learn more. Unfortunately, it has never been my good fortune to have a student who wishes to learn anything."

"A field of force, hah?" said Remo.

Chiun nodded. "It is why everything works," he said. "Why do you think that women react to you as that nurse did in the hospital? Certainly not because you are the beautiful person of her dreams because you are too tall and your skin is dead pasty white wrong color, and your hair is black and you have too much of it and you have the big nose that all you white people have. No, it is not because of your beauty."

"I have a beautiful heart," Remo said. "When I was in the orphanage, even when I got into trouble, the nuns would tell me I had a beautiful heart and soul."

"Nuns," Chiun said. "These are the ladies who always wear mourning garments, even when no one has died, and always wear wedding rings, even though they are not married?"

"That's right," Remo said.

"*They* would think you have a beautiful heart," Chiun said. "That child in the hospital was in your field of force and she felt the pressure of it all over her body and she did not know how to deal with it, never having experienced it before. It was like the touching of many hands on her body all at once."

"A psychic massage," Remo said. "You mean I give the little chickies a rubdown without ever raising a hand?"

"If you wish to be gross about it, and of course you do, that is correct," Chiun said.

"And signals rebound back and if I worked harder I could read those signals?"

"Also correct. It is most important that you study and learn this quickly."

"Why?" asked Remo, surprised because Chiun generally gave instructions and lessons as if Remo had another fifty years of study ahead of him.

"Because those two are racing toward us right now," Chiun said, "and if you do not soon defend yourself, I will have to start looking for a new pupil."

Remo spun about as the two men were closing in.

114

One ran heavily, favoring his left leg. The other glided smoothly, with the same kind of natural grace that Remo himself had had years ago when he was just an ordinary man. The limper had a knife. The other man had a blackjack. They were wearing plaid lumber jackets over white pants.

The man with the knife raised it over his head as he ran and as he reached Remo, plunged it downward toward Remo's left shoulder.

Remo drew his shoulder back so the knife missed by a fraction of an inch and then spun on his heel into a 360-degree turn. As he spun, he saw Chiun ambling away toward the entrance of a penny arcade.

As Remo finished his spin, he raised his left foot and took the blackjack out of the right hand of the smooth moving one. The blackjack fell to the ground with a thud. The athletic one bent down for it and his hand closed on the grip, just as Remo's heel closed on his hand. There was a sound like chicken bones breaking.

The man yelped. The other man with the knife lifted it again over his head and spiked it down at Remo's face. The knifepoint stopped a quarter inch from Remo's face as the man's arm was halted by Remo's upflung wrist. The shockwaves sent pain up the man's arm, radiating down into the base of his spine. For the first time in fifteen years, ever since he had been taken out of the National Football League by a crackback block, his left knee hurt. He had only an instant to savor the hurt because suddenly he felt a burning sensation in his stomach and the skinny man's fingers were buried in it, up to his wrist, and the football player could feel his organs

115

mashed and he felt like a windup toy slowing down as the spring played out. The inner tension of his body slowed down.

Slower. Slower. Slower.

Stop.

The man dropped to the sidewalk. The other man yanked his hand out from under Remo's foot, grabbed the blackjack in his left hand and swung again at Remo's head. Remo slipped under the blow, slapped his hand upward against the man's elbow and instead of stopping his blow when it missed the target, the man felt his arm speeding up and the blackjack winging toward his own temple; he did not have the presence of mind to open his hand and drop the weapon before it crushed his temple bone.

The man tried to scream, could not, then sipped air as he fell to the pavement over the body of the other man.

Remo looked down at the two of them. Their jackets had fallen open and he saw that they wore white jackets that matched their white slacks. Like hospital uniforms, he thought. Neither man stirred and Remo cursed his bad luck. If he had thought of it, he would have kept one of them alive to answer questions.

A man and a woman walked down the street toward Remo and the two men at his feet. Without ever really looking, they separated and passed the tableau, one on each side, and then joined hands again on the other side and continued strolling.

A policeman approached. He stood alongside Remo and looked down at the two bodies.

"Dead?" he asked.

"I guess so," Remo said.

"You going to want to report this?" the cop asked.

"Should I?" asked Remo.

"Well, you can, you know. I mean, two muggers attacked you and you killed them. I know a lot of police departments don't mind getting reports on things like that."

"But you do?"

"Look at it this way, pal," said the policeman earnestly. He leaned close to Remo and Remo read his identification plate.

Patrolman L. Blade said "If you report it, then I'm going to have to make a lot of reports and things, triplicate and like that." As he spoke, pedestrians continued to walk by without stopping, taking great pains not to look directly at the dead men on the sidewalk. "And they'll take your name and address and then you'll have to go before a grand jury and who knows what the hell might happen, maybe they'll indict you."

"For protecting myself?"

"This is New York. You've got to understand how we feel about things like that," said Patrolman L. Blade. "Actually, I'm on your side. I guess, maybe, half us cops are. But if we let people go around getting the idea that they can protect themselves, that they've got a right to protect themselves, well, where does that leave the patrolmen's benevolent association?"

"In other words," said Remo, "protecting yourself against a mugger without being in the policeman's union is like scabbing the job?"

"That's right," Patrolman L. Blade said.

"I see," said Remo. "I'd like to know who these guys are."

"Let's give them a toss," the cop said. He bent

over the bodies. Practiced hands moved through their pockets swiftly. Neither man carried a wallet or any type of identification.

"Sorry. No ID," the policeman said.

"If I report this, the bodies go to the morgue?"

The policeman nodded.

"And they identify them from fingerprints, right?"

"In theory," Patrolman L. Blade said.

"What do you mean, in theory?"

"We've got so many bodies that it takes a couple of months to get to them. You want identities, figure sixty to ninety days. If everything goes smooth."

"What happens if I don't make a report?"

"Nothing."

"What do you mean, nothing?" Remo asked.

"You and me, we just go on about our business like nothing happened."

"And what happens to them?" Remo asked, pointing down.

"They'll be gone by morning," the cop said.

"But what happens to them?"

"I don't know. I just know that they're always gone by morning. Maybe medical schools take them for experiments." He winked at Remo. "Maybe pervoes need them for dirty things. I don't know. They ain't my unions."

"God help us," Remo said. "Do what you want." He turned to walk to the amusement arcade.

The cop called him. "Hey, buddy," he said.

"What?"

"Remember. You never talked to me. I don't know nothing."

"Truer words were never spoken," Remo said.

Inside the high-ceilinged arcade, Chiun was nego-

118

tiating change of a dollar with the clerk. They both looked up in relief as Remo approached.

"Remo, will you tell this idiot that that dollar bill is a silver certificate and worth more than four quarters?" Chiun said.

"He's telling you the truth," Remo told the clerk.

The clerk shook his head. "All I know is my boss wouldn't like it, I give more than four quarters change for a dollar."

"Invincible ignorance," Chiun said.

Remo took a dollar out of his pocket and gave it to the clerk. The clerk returned the silver certificate. Chiun had it it out of Remo's hands and back among the folds of his robe before Remo's eyes had a chance to focus on the bill.

"I owe you a dollar," Chiun said.

"I'll remind you," Remo said. He asked the clerk which was the toughest machine.

"South Sea Dreams in the back," the young man said. "Never given up a game yet."

Remo walked with Chiun to the back and showed him how to insert the money and explained the purpose of the game. Chiun seemed offended that one did not win cash prizes.

Two young men in black leather jackets smirked at each other when they heard Chiun talk. They were playing the machine next to his.

Remo told them: "This gentleman's going to play this machine. Save yourself a lot of trouble and leave him alone."

"Yeah? Who says so?"

"Pal, I'm just trying to save you grief. Leave him alone."

"Yeah. Who says so?"

Remo sighed. "Have it your own way."

There was a telephone booth outside the arcade which vandals had not yet turned into a public urinal, and Remo called Smith's nighttime number. Smith answered the telephone on the first ring.

"What's the latest on Lippincott?" asked Remo.

"Holding steady. But no one can find out what's wrong," Smith said.

"Chiun says it's some kind of poison," said Remo.

"They can't find any foreign substances in his blood," Smith said.

"If Chiun says it's poison, it's poison."

"Have you found out anything?" Smith asked.

"Nothing really," Remo said. "Oh, two guys tried to kill us on the street."

"Who are they?"

"Were," said Remo. "I don't know. They didn't have IDs. But, Smitty, . . ."

"Yes?"

"They were wearing hospital clothes. I'm thinking there's some kind of medical tie-in with this thing. Can you run that through the computers?"

"I'll check it out," Smith said.

Remo looked through the window of the arcade. The two young men with leather jackets and greasy fifties' hair were standing on either side of Chiun, talking to each other across the machine. Chiun seemed not to pay attention. Remo shook his head and turned away. He didn't want to watch.

"Any word from Ruby?" asked Remo.

"None yet."

"Good," said Remo. "When she calls in, tell her we'll have this whole thing cleaned up before she even figures out what it's about. Tell her I said so."

"You sure you want me to say that?" asked Smith.

"Yeah," said Remo. "Well . . . maybe not. I'll call you tomorrow."

When he went back inside, the two youths in leather jackets were standing on tiptoe on either side of Chiun, straining upward. Remo saw why. Chiun had them by the index fingers and was using their fingers to operate the flippers of the pinball machines.

"I warned you," he said to the two as he approached.

"Make him let us go," one squealed.

"Let them go, Chiun," said Remo.

"Not until this game is done," said Chiun. "They graciously volunteered to show me how it is played."

"I'll bet they did. What ball are you on?" Remo asked.

"I am playing my first ball," Chiun said.

"Still?" asked Remo.

"It is perfectly good," said Chiun. "I see no reason to use another ball."

And because Remo knew that it might be days before Chiun used all five balls of the game, he pressed his hip against the pinball machine and then hit it sideways.

The machine's scoring lights went out. The "Tilt" sign lit up.

"What happened?" said Chiun.

"The machine tilted," Remo said.

Chiun pressed the two young men's fingers against the flipper buttons. The flippers did not work.

"What is this tilt?" he asked.

"That means the game's over," said Remo.

"How did that happen?" asked Chiun.

"Sometimes it just happens," Remo said.

"Yeah," said one of the young men. "So let us go, will you, please, sir?"

Chiun nodded and released the two youths. They began trying to rub the pain from their fingers.

"The next time some gentle soul comes in seeking a moment's diversion from the cares of his life, I advise you to leave him alone," Chiun said.

"Yes, sir."

"We will, sir."

Chiun walked away. Remo followed him. At the door, Chiun said "I saw you tilt that machine by hitting it with your hip."

"Sorry about that, Chiun," Remo said.

"It is all right. I might have been there for days finishing that game, and it is a singularly stupid way to spend one's time, if you cannot win money."

When he returned from the Upper East Side Clinic where his son Randall still lay unconscious, Elmer Lippincott walked heavily up the steps to his bedroom. He didn't relish what he was about to do, but he had lived his entire life doing what he had to do. It was his code of conduct.

He wondered. How do you tell a woman you love something that might destroy her love for you?

"You just tell her," he mumbled half-aloud, to himself as he walked leadenly down the upstairs hallway. It was a hall undistinguished by paintings. Others as rich as Lippincott might have had a hallway lined with oil portraits of their ancestors but Elmer Lippincott's ancestors had been dirt farmers and cowpunchers and once in jest he had said that while they weren't exactly the scum of the earth, they weren't exactly the salt either.

122

He heard laughter from inside his bedroom as he reached the door so he knocked lightly once, before walking inside.

His wife, Gloria, was sitting up in her bed wearing a satin gown, a sheet tucked demurely around her body. On the little stool at the dressing table sat Dr. Jesse Beers. They had obviously been sharing a joke because they looked a little startled and if Lippincott's mind had been working more clearly, he might have thought they even looked a little guilty as he walked in.

Dr. Beers blew his nose in a handkerchief and seemed to take the occasion to wipe his face thoroughly. Gloria was not as immaculate as she usually was. One strap of her nightgown was off her shoulder and the rising swell of her left breast was visible. Her lipstick seemed slightly smeared. Lippincott noticed none of these things.

Beers finished wiping his face and stood as Lippincott came in. The doctor was a tall broad-shouldered, young man.

"How's the patient, Doctor?" asked Lippincott.

"Fine, sir. Top notch."

"Good." Lippincott smiled at his wife and without looking back said, "Doctor, would you excuse us?"

"Of course. Goodnight, Mrs. Lippincott. Sir."

After he closed the door behind him, Lippincott said to his wife: "Nice fella."

"If you like the type," Gloria said. She opened her arms wide and extended them toward her husband in an invitation to join her on the bed.

Lippincott tossed his jacket over a chair as he walked toward her. God, he loved her. And soon she'd be the mother of his child. Hopefully, a son. A real son. As he sat on the bed, her arms and eyes were so inviting, her look so loving, that he again felt a shudder at what he had to do. He closed his big rawboned hand around one of hers.

"What's the matter, Elmer?" she asked.

"You see right through me, don't you?"

"I don't know about that," Gloria said. "But I can see when something's on your mind. You come in here all sour and Walter Brennan looking and I know something's wrong."

He smiled despite himself, but the smile was just a flash across his face and then there was nothing there except hurt and pain.

"You'd better tell me about it," Gloria said. "It can't be as bad as your face makes it look."

"It is," Lippincott said. "It is."

He waited for her to say something. When she didn't answer, the silence seemed to fill the room like a pressure. He turned away and faced the hall door as he spoke.

"I want you to know, first of all, that I love you and our baby," he said.

"I know that," Gloria said. She touched her fingers to the back of his head, swirling them through his thick white hair.

"I used to love my . . . my boys that same way," Lippincott said. "Until I found out, thanks to Dr. Gladstone, that they weren't mine. Three sons my wife gave me. Sons of some other man. Or men." His voice broke.

"Elmer, this is all old ground we've covered before," Gloria said. "Why do we have to do it again? You can't do anything about the past, about some

124

woman who treated you badly and is dead now anyway. Forgive and forget."

He turned back to her. There was a tear in the corner of his right eye. "I wish I had done that," he said. "But I couldn't. My pride was hurt too much. And then I was angry and vengeful. You know those experiments Dr. Gladstone does up at the laboratory?"

"Not really," Gloria said. "Science doesn't interest me."

"Well, she works with animals to produce substances that can be used in people to affect their behavior. It's how she cured my impotence. Well, I asked her to . . . to use some of those formulas on Lem and Randall and Douglas."

Gloria's eyes opened wide. Lippincott shook his head sadly.

"I didn't really want to hurt them," he said. "I just wanted to . . . to pay them back . . . to show them how much they owed to the Lippincott name."

"It wasn't their fault, Elmer. They didn't have anything to do with how their mother acted."

"I know that now. But too late. I wanted to embarrass them. But the medicine was too much for Lem and now he's dead. And tonight . . . well, Randall's in a hospital, almost dead. My fault. I just came from there."

Gloria moved forward on the bed and put her arms around Lippincott, cradling him to her shoulder.

"Oh, honey," she said. "I'm so sorry. But you mustn't feel guilty. That won't solve anything."

"But Lem is dead," he said.

"That's right. He's dead and there's nothing any-body can do about it. Except grieve."

"And feel guilty," Lippincott said. Tears were roll-ing fully down his face now, coursing through the crags and folds of his dry weathered skin.

"No," Gloria said firmly. "Guilt does nothing for anyone. What you can do is try your best to see that Randall gets well. And, even though it sounds cruel, you can just forget Lem. You will, you know, in time. Try to do it now. Spare yourself the anguish. Forget him. Do it for me. For our new son. Your son."

"You think I can?"

"I know you can," Gloria said. Lippincott took her in his arms for a moment, then settled her back onto her pillow. He reached for the telephone.

"I've told Dr. Gladstone to stop," he said. "Enough is enough."

"I'm glad," she said.

He spoke into the telephone. "Dr. Beers, would you come in here please?"

Beers arrived a few seconds later. He was still wearing his tweed slacks and quiana shirt.

"Yes, sir," he said.

"Dr. Beers, my son Randall is in the Upper East Side Clinic in Manhattan. I want you to go down there, and to consult with your associate Dr. Glad-stone, and do what is necessary to make sure that Randall recovers."

"What's wrong with him, sir?" Beers asked. He looked, as if in confusion, from Lippincott to the young and beautiful Gloria.

"Dr. Gladstone will know," Lippincott said. "So please go now."

"And Mrs. Lippincott?" Beers asked.

"I'll be here. She'll be all right. If there's anything wrong, I'll call you immediately."

"I'll leave right away," Beers said. He left the room.

"And now everything will be all right," Gloria told her husband. "So you just take those clothes off and come to bed. I'm going to the bathroom."

She locked the bathroom door behind her, turned the water on fast, then picked up the telephone on the wall next to the sink.

She dialed three digits.

When the telephone was picked up, she spoke two words: "Kill him."

She hung up the telephone, washed her hands and went back to her husband.

After Randall, she thought, there were only two Lippincotts to go. The third son, Douglas.

And, of course, the old man.

Elmer Lippincott took the news from Dr. Beers very hard. His son, Randall, had expired in the night. Neither he nor Dr. Gladstone had been able to do anything about it.

"One moment he was fine. And the next moment, he stopped breathing. I'm sorry, Mr. Lippincott."

"You're not to blame," Lippincott said. "I am." His heart was heavy until breaking. Fortunately, his young wife Gloria comforted him, and then she went to sleep.

Very soundly.

CHAPTER ELEVEN

Ruby couldn't sleep. Even at 2 A.M., the traffic noises in the street below her hotel window annoyed her. The whirring of the heater in the room annoyed her. And the thought that Remo might be ahead of her in this case annoyed her most of all.

She turned on the bed lamp and dialed Smith's home number. The special telephone was installed in Smith's bedroom. It had no bell and when a call came in, a small red light flashed at the base of the receiver. Smith, who had spent his maturing years with the O.S.S. and then with the CIA, before being selected to head CURE, slept so lightly the red flash woke him instantly.

He lifted the phone off the base, listened for a moment to his wife's heavy regular snoring, and whispered: "Hold on, please."

He put the call on hold, then picked it up on another telephone in the bathroom.

"Smith," he said.

"This is Ruby. I'm sorry for calling you so late but I couldn't sleep."

"Neither could I," Smith lied. He did not like to make people feel uncomfortable. Uncomfortable people took longer to get to the point. "Have you learned anything?" he asked.

"Well, I'm glad I didn't wake you," Ruby said. "Remember that detective, Meadows? He's definitely the one who wrote the letter to The Man. And he's been missing for about two weeks. The plot against the Lippincotts has something to do with someplace on the East Side. Called Lifeline Laboratory. And there was another guy with Meadows."

"How'd you find this out?" Smith asked.

"I got my hands on Meadows's throwaway sheets when he was writing that letter. They had more information than the letter did."

"What do you think happened to Meadows?"

"My guess is that he bought the farm," Ruby said.

"It would seem likely," Smith said.

"What about the dodo? He find anything?"

"Remo? A little, but it ties in with what you told me." Quickly, Smith filled her in on the attempt to murder Remo and Chiun, and the poisoning of Randall Lippincott, and the fact that the two men who attacked Remo and Chiun were wearing hospital type clothing. Remo suggested a medical tie-in among the Lippincotts.

"Shoot, he getting close," Ruby said.

"I put it in the computers before I left Folcroft," Smith said. "Hold on."

He pressed the hold button and dialed a number that connected directly into the massive computer banks at Folcroft Sanitarium, CURE's headquarters. A mechanical computer voice answered. Smith pushed the buttons on the telephone receiver in a numerical pattern that triggered the computer's readout mechanism. The computer voice recited some information mechanically to Smith, who hung up after first saying his habitual Thank You before picking up Ruby's call again.

"You're right," he told her. "Lifeline Laboratory is funded by Lippincott money. It's headed by two doctors, Elena Gladstone and Loren Beers. They are also private physicians who treat the Lippincott family."

"What they do at the laboratory?" Ruby asked.

"Some kind of esoteric research. Behavioral studies."

"Esoteric?" asked Ruby.

"Far out," explained Smith.

"Got it. Where's the dodo staying?"

Smith gave Ruby Remo's hotel.

"What are you going to do now?" he asked.

"I was going to visit the laboratory."

"I wouldn't recommend your going there alone. Contact Remo," Smith said.

"He dumb," Ruby said. "He can't find anything out. He'll go barging in and messing up everything, breaking furniture and playing the fool. Then we never find out anything."

"Now you know the cross I've had to bear," Smith said patiently. "But I don't want anything to happen to you."

He was silent. There was a pause at the other end of the line.

"All right," Ruby said. "I'll get together with Remo."

"Good," said Smith. "Keep in touch."

He hung up. Ruby hung up and said softly to herself: "Booshit." She sat on the edge of the bed. It wasn't that she didn't like Remo. She did. In fact,

131

sometimes she tingled when she thought of him and if it hadn't been for the fact that Chiun was always trying to push them into bed together so they could produce a tan baby for him, she and Remo probably would have gotten it on by now.

Now, that would be a baby, Ruby thought. Homo superior. If it got Remo's physical ability and her brains. But what if the baby had Remo's brains? What a burden to lay on a child.

She'd worry about that when the time came.

Ruby dressed quickly and checked the wallet inside her large pocketbook to make sure she was carrying the right kind of identification. Downstairs, she called a cab.

"City morgue," she told the driver.

"Gee, lady," he said. "You don't have to commit suicide. I'll marry you."

"I already got one loser," Ruby said. "Drive."

Her Justice Department identification got her through the string of clerks that manned the morgue, even at 2:45 A.M. New York might be bankrupt, but they never seemed to run out of money to hire more clerks, she realized. At the morgue, she passed through seven layers of personnel before she finally got to what was called "the storage room."

A bored policeman checked her identification carefully, moving his lips as he read it, then asked her who she was looking for. The cop smelled of cheap whiskey. His belt pressed into his huge belly like a knife into an unbaked biscuit. Ruby wondered whose brother-in-law he was to get a job indoors in winter.

She took a picture of Zack Meadows from her pocketbook.

"This one," she said.

"I don't recognize him," the cop said. "But a lot of them don't look like much anymore. When'd he come in?"

Ruby shrugged. "Sometime in the last two weeks."

"Oh, jeez," the policeman said. "Can't you narrow it down any more than that?"

"No," Ruby said, "I can't. How many unidentified bodies you got coming in in the last two weeks anyway?"

"A couple of dozen, for Christ sake. This ain't Connecticut, you know. This is New York."

"Yeah, I know," said Ruby. "Let's look at them."

The bodies were kept in lockers with large stainless steel doors. They were put in head first. Each body was covered with a sheet and there were cardboard tags tied to the left big toe. With bodies that had been identified, the tags carried that information. Name, age, address. With unidentified bodies, the tags carried when and where the body was found and referred back to a police file number. Most of the unidentified dead were victims of gunshot wounds.

"Don't you send prints to Washington for identification?" Ruby asked the cop, as she shook her head "no" and he slid another corpse back into the freezer locker. The overhead lighting was bright, nonglare fluorescent. She was able to see the faces very clearly.

"Sure. When we get around to it. But we got a lot of things to do and we don't always get around to it in a hurry. This is New York, you know."

"Yeah," Ruby said. "I know. It ain't Connecticut."

"Right."

She found Zack Meadows in the sixth locker. There was no mistaking the bloated face. Looking down at him, covered only by a sheet, his hair matted around his head as if he had died stepping out of the shower, Ruby thought to herself that even in death, Zack Meadows looked stupid. She bit her lip. You shouldn't talk bad of the dead, her mother had always told her. God would punish you for that. She inspected the corpse carefully. The fingertips on both hands were destroyed. They looked as if they had been cut off.

"That's unusual, isn't it?" she said.

"What?" asked the cop.

Ruby pointed to Meadows' fingers. The cop shrugged.

"Who knows?" he said.

The tag on Meadows's toe said he had been taken out of Central Park's lake, with another body, two weeks before.

"Where's the other body?" she said.

"Let's see." The patrolman looked at the tag. "It ought to say on the tag but it don't. I don't know what the hell help is coming to when they can't do a simple thing like put the right information on a toe tag. The kind of people we get around here."

"Where might the other body be?" Ruby asked patiently.

"Around here somewhere," he said angrily. "You done with this one?"

"Yeah."

The cop slammed the rolling tray back into the freezer locker. It hit the back wall with a loud metallic clank. God help Zack Meadows, Ruby thought, at the hands of this cretin.

The cop began to pull out slabs quickly, just checking the toe information. On the fourth try, he found it.

"Here it is," he said. "Central Park lake. Same day. That's it. Want to see him?"

"Yes," Ruby said.

He pulled out the tray and pulled down the sheet from the face. It was a small man with thinning hair and a mousey meek face. Ruby checked his hands. His fintertips too had been cut off.

"Probably two guys got a load on and got into a swimming contest and both of them drownded," the cop said.

"In December?" Ruby said.

"Could be. Remember, this . . ."

"I know. It ain't Connecticut," Ruby said. "What do you make of their fingertips being mutilated?"

"I don't make nothing of it," the policeman said.

No wonder the city was like Fort Apache, Ruby thought. She gave the small corpse an encouraging slap on the bottom of its bare foot, then smiled at the cop.

"Thanks. You've been a big help," she said.

"All right," he said. "Maybe you can do something for me some day."

"Hope so," Ruby said. Like put a tag on your toe, she thought.

Out front, Ruby caught another cab and gave it the name of Remo's hotel. Inside the hotel, the desk clerk looked at her as if she were a hooker on her way to visit a john with a middle-of-the-night urge.

135

She rode a squeaking elevator up to the twenty-third floor and stood outside Remo's door. She found a pen and paper in her purse and wrote a note.

Chiun heard the noise instantly. Something had been pushed under their door. He rose quietly from the grass mat on which he slept. Remo was asleep in the inside bedroom. Chiun saw the piece of paper on the floor. He opened the note and looked at it. The greeting read: "Dear Dodo." Chiun decided the note was not for him. He crumpled it onto the floor and went back to his mat to return to sleep. He hoped the squeaking of the elevator did not keep him awake all night.

Back in the lobby, the clerk again looked at Ruby with distaste. Once he could have gotten away with; twice was too much.

Ruby walked up to the desk and even though the clerk was standing directly in front of her, she slammed her hand down on the night service bell, sending a loud ring throughout the lobby.

"What was that for?" the clerk asked in his best surly manner.

"Just making sure you alive," Ruby said.

"And now that you're sure . . ."

"Who says I'm sure?" Ruby asked. "All I see is somebody staring down his long nose and making sounds."

The clerk took a breath. "What is it, Miss, that you want? We don't want people hanging around the lobby, if you get my drift."

Ruby dug her wallet from her purse and opened it to a New York City police identity card.

"That elevator over there ain't been inspected in the last six months like it's supposed to be," she said.

The clerk looked startled. He stammered. "Just an oversight, I'm sure."

"People get killed by oversights," Ruby said. "If I look at all the rest of them elevators, you think they'll have oversights too?"

"I . . . er . . . I don't know."

"Well, I'm going to take it easy on you. I won't be back till noon. Make sure those elevators are checked by then 'cause if they ain't, I'm going to close them all down and you can have your guests walk upstairs. You get my drift?"

"Yes, ma'am."

CHAPTER TWELVE

Dr. Elena Gladstone had not been able to get back to sleep in her apartment above the Lifeline Laboratory.

She had felt relieved when Dr. Jesse Beers called her to let her know that he had "taken care" of Randall Lippincott before the man had a chance to talk.

"Better late than never," she had told him.

But what kept her awake was a telephone call she did not receive and as the clock moved on toward 4 A.M., she began to doubt if she was ever again going to hear from the two men she had sent after the Oriental and the American. They should have been back by now, but they had not returned and they had not called and inside she had the sinking feeling that perhaps the two government agents—what were their names, Remo and Chiun?—just perhaps there was more to them than met the eye. They had managed to keep Randall Lippincott alive, when by all medical practice he should have been dead. How had they done it? It had caused no real danger. Jesse Beers had taken care of it, but still those two were a threat. For a brief moment, a chill passed through her body and she thought that perhaps she might be willing to get out of the whole business.

She rejected that thought right away. She wasn't talking about wealth; she was thinking about riches. Not just millions, but hundreds of millions. She was thinking of yachts and villas and chauffeurs and the beautiful life.

Nothing must get in the way of that dream.

Ruby saw the silent alarm wires in the back door of the laboratory, so she did not attempt to slip the door. She rooted around inside her pocketbook and found a long wire with two thin adhesive clips on the ends. She carefully pressed the clips into the top of the door, until she was able to bridge the two wires of the alarm.

Then she picked the lock with a small tool from a set she carried with her.

"CIA was good for something," she mumbled to herself.

She stood inside the closed door of the laboratory for long minutes, waiting, ready to flee if another alarm had sounded and alerted someone. Her eyes grew accustomed to the dark. She saw the cages lining the wall, cages of rats and mice and monkeys. She examined them clinically. While most people might be afraid of rats and mice, in the neighborhood where Ruby had grown up, they were constant companions, and you didn't stay emotionally fearful of them for long. When Ruby was ten years old, a rat had climbed into her bed and bitten her. She had grabbed it behind the head, and beaten it to death with the spiked heel of her mother's shoe.

The animals quieted as Ruby stood in the room. She listened. Had Zack Meadows been here too? Had he come to find out what was going on, only to wind up dead in the Central Park lake? If that was what had happened, Ruby realized she had better be very careful.

There was no point in trying to sleep anymore so Elena Gladstone dressed casually in blue jeans and a plaid shirt and decided to go down to the laboratory to look in on her latest experiments. She had succeeded in conditioning a rat to be afraid of metal, to the point that the rat went berserk if placed in a metal cage. Even after hundreds of experiments, she never lost her sense of wonder that a learned response such as fear, trained into an animal, would produce a substance in the animal's brain that could be isolated, purified, and intensified so that it could be injected into the bloodstream of another animal and produce exactly the same fear.

She had gotten into the research a decade before when, just out of medical school, she had taken a job in a laboratory and been exposed to the famous flatworm experiments, in which flatworms were trained to respond to light. Then the trained worms were cut up and fed to other flatworms who immediately developed the same response to the light stimulus.

The eccentric doctor for whom she worked had been inclined to dismiss the experiment as a curiosity but it became the pivot of Dr. Elena Gladstone's life. She never published any of her findings or original research. Somehow, in the back of her mind, there had always been a feeling that there was a profit to be turned through this research and this profit would be in direct proportion to how much she knew and how little others knew.

She was dressed and, barefooted, started down-stairs.

Ruby had seen the guard sitting just inside the front door of the building, and she had seen a small office off to the side of the main laboratory room. She went into the office and struck a match, to satisfy herself that the room had a window through which she could escape if it became necessary.

She closed the door behind her, locked it, opened the window, and went over to the desk. The name-plate read "Dr. Gladstone."

Ruby switched on the desk lamp and turned her attention to the filing cabinet behind the desk.

It was locked but her lock picks quickly opened it. She whistled softly to herself as the top drawer opened. In the back of the drawer were patient folders and there were the Lippincotts. Elmer, Lem, Douglas, and Randall. She moved the desk lamp closer to the file cabinet, then spun around in the swivel chair so she could read the reports more easily.

Elena Gladstone casually unlocked the door to the laboratory, stepped inside, then froze against the wall. At the end of the hallway, light was pouring from her office. Silently, she walked down the hall, pressed close to the wall. She peered in through a corner of the window in the door. There was a woman inside, a black woman with an Afro, sitting at the cabinet, reading her files. Behind the desk, the solitary window in the office was open, obviously for fast escape if it became necessary.

Who was she, Elena wondered. Perhaps she had

142

some relationship to that private detective who had come snooping around a few weeks before.

Noiseless on her bare feet, Elena moved away from the door and went back out the front door of the laboratory. In a hallway closet, she found what she was looking for, secreted the small can inside her shirt and walked to the front of the building.

The guard looked up when she approached. As if stricken by guilt, he tried to hide his copy of *Hustler* Magazine under some papers on the desk.

"Hello, Doctor," he said. "What are you doing up?"

"Just walking around, thinking," she said. "This is what I want you to do."

She explained it very carefully, then had Herman repeat it. He did not understand his instructions but he nodded and said he would do just what she ordered.

Dr. Gladstone walked outside into the cold December air and as she stepped outside, behind her, Herman began counting softly to himself, "One thousand and one, one thousand and two, one thousand and . . ."

When the count had reached sixty, Herman stood up. Whistling loudly, he walked toward the laboratory door in the rear of the building. Even though the door was unlocked, he fumbled with the knob for awhile, then reached inside and flipped on the laboratory light.

In Dr. Gladstone's office, Ruby had heard the whistling and turned off the desk lamp. In the dark, she had replaced the Lippincott folders in the rear of the file cabinet. She stood near the open window,

143

waiting. She heard the fumbling with the doorknob in the outer office, and then her office was semi-lit as the lightswitch outside was turned on.

Ruby didn't wait to see the guard follow the last of his instructions, which were to turn around, go back to his desk, put on his coat and go home early.

Ruby stepped up on a book case to hoist herself through the window. Her body was halfway out when Elena Gladstone stepped out of the shadows alongside the building.

As Ruby looked up and saw her, Dr. Gladstone raised a can of Mace and sprayed it in Ruby's face. It hit the young black women like a punch, taking the wind out of her lungs. She could feel it tingling on her face and the burning sensation in her eyes, and then she could feel her body start to grow numb and her fingers slipped from the windowsill and Ruby fell back inside, on the office floor, unconscious.

Elena Gladstone, stepping carefully in her barefeet, so she did not step on glass or sharp pebbles, came back around the front of the building. She checked to make sure that the guard had gone, locked the door behind her and walked into her office, to see just what she had captured.

Remo was up before the sun and when he stepped out into the living room of the hotel suite, he saw Chiun lying in a pink sleeping kimono on the grass mat, his hands folded steeple-like in front of him, staring at the ceiling.

"What's the matter, Chiun? Trouble sleeping?"

"Yes," said Chiun.

"Sorry," said Remo.

144

"You should be," said Chiun as he rose to a sitting position.

"I didn't have anything to do with it," Remo said. "I don't snore. And I keep the door to the bedroom closed so you won't complain about my breathing or the springs in the bed squeaking or anything like that. Find yourself another patsy."

"A lot you know," Chiun said. "Who was it who put us in a hotel where the elevator squeaks? And if people were not always coming to this floor to look for you, the elevator would not always be squeaking and keeping me awake."

"Looking for me? Who?" Remo asked.

"And if people were not always slipping messages for you under the door, I might just be able to get some rest," Chiun said.

Remo saw the crumpled note on the floor. He smoothed it out and read it aloud:

"Dear Dodo. What you're looking for is Lifeline Laboratory on East Eighty-first Street. Ruby."

He looked at Chiun. "When'd this come?"

"You're not going to ask me how I knew it was for you?"

"No. When'd it come?"

"Who knows? Two hours ago. An hour ago."

"And you read it and didn't do anything? Ruby's probably gone to this place and she might be in trouble."

"One, I did not read it because it was not addressed to me. I am not 'Dear Dodo.' Two, if that Ruby woman wrote it and is going wherever that place is, she will not be in trouble because she can take care of herself, that one, which is why she would make a fine mother for someone's son, if someone had but the brains to see that, but one cannot expect too much of a stone."

Remo was on the telephone to Smith and when the light flashed, Smith's wife was downstairs preparing breakfast so Smith spoke from his bedroom.

"Yes, Remo. The Lifeline Laboratory. I told her to alert you before she went there. All right. Keep me advised."

When he hung up with Remo, Smith turned the receiver of the phone upside down to expose a panel of buttons. With practiced fingers, he pressed a 10-digit sequence. There was no buzzing ring of the phone. There was only silence for thirty seconds and then a voice said "Yes, Dr. Smith."

"On the Lippincott matter, our people are closing in," Smith said.

"Thank you," said the President of the United States as Smith hung up.

CHAPTER THIRTEEN

It was a pain in the neck.

Ruby knew it was a pain in the neck and as she struggled toward consciousness, her mind asked what was a pain in the neck. Remo. Remo was a pain in the neck. Working for the government was a pain in the neck. If she had had any sense, she never would have gotten involved with the CIA and then with CURE. She would have just kept running the Afro wig shop in Norfolk, Virginia, building her business, moving on to other things, and socking enough money away to retire by thirty.

Not her, though. She had to be smart and work for the government. That was the pain in the neck. And Remo, he was a pain in the neck. Chiun and Smith, pains in the neck. Her brother, Lucius. No, he wasn't a pain in the neck. He was a pain in the ass.

Her eyes opened and the pain in her neck was real. It felt like the bite of a June bottle fly and she tried to move her right hand up to the left side of her throat to touch the sore spot but she couldn't. She craned her head and saw that her right hand was strapped down. So was the left hand. So was she. She was lying on a hospital cot, with thick broad bands of canvas holding her down she she couldn't move. And it all came back to her. The Mace in the face as she tried to escape. And there, across the room, hanging up the telephone was Dr. Elena Gladstone who had a broad smile on her face as she turned toward Ruby and walked toward her. The room was brightly lighted with overhead fluorescent fixtures. Ruby had seen that kind of lighting somewhere recently. Where? She shuddered as she remembered. In the city morgue, when she was examining corpses.

"How are you feeling, Miss Gonzalez?"

"How'd you know my name?" asked Ruby.

"I know a great deal about you. Your name. Who you work for. What you do. The identities of the American and the Oriental who have been bothering me. Your suspicions about the Lippincott tragedies and the death of Mr. Meadows."

"You drugged me," Ruby said. It was not a question, but more a silent grudging acceptance of an unpleasant fact.

"Yes, dear, I did. Now how would you like to die?

"Either of two ways," Ruby said. "Not much and not at all."

"Neither of those is acceptable," Dr. Gladstone said. "We'll have to find something better."

"Take your time. I'm in no hurry." Ruby's cautious cat's eyes had prowled the entire room. The walls of the room were lined with more cages, holding rats and hamsters. She saw a scalpel on a table across the room. Maybe there was a chance.

"You seem to have figured out everything about me," Ruby said. "I'm sure impressed by all that science stuff, but I can't figure out what you're doing at all."

"It's not surprising," Dr. Gladstone said. "Few could."

Pickaninny wouldn't work, Ruby decided. Maybe vanity.

"The advances you've made with peptides are really a breakthrough," Ruby said.

Dr. Gladstone's eyebrows lifted. "Peptides? My, you are well read."

Ruby nodded and ignored the patronizing. "I just don't understand how you can synthesize compounds from one species and make them work in a totally different species."

The redheaded doctor's eyes sparkled with interest. "I don't synthesize them. I use natural compounds. What I synthesized and what made it all work, was . . . well, you recall in organ transplants, the necessity to use anti-rejection medicines so organs from one person would be accept by another's body?"

"I remember," Ruby said.

"I synthesized the basic components that prevent rejection, and found out how to bind those to the peptide compounds. I can move substances from one species to another with one hundred percent effectiveness."

"Incredible," Ruby said. "What got me too was the range of responses you can program. I can see training an animal to be afraid of the dark or of water. But of Orientals? Of clothing or restraints? That's amazing."

"Not really. It's just the natural outgrowth of simple behavioral training. Use an Oriental assistant to abuse animals. When you inflict pain on him, make sure his environment is yellow-colored. They will react soon enough. Clothing? You just couple some kind of blanket with electric shock. Then switch to other fabric coverings. Before long, the rats learn. Anything covering them means a painful jolt of electricity, and that knowledge creates peptide compounds in the brain, and those can make a man afraid of the same thing."

"Like Randall Lippincott?" asked Ruby.

"Exactly like Randall Lippincott," Dr. Gladstone's eyes narrowed as she realized the woman strapped to the hospital cot in front of her was still the enemy.

"But why? Why the Lippincotts?" asked Ruby.

"Because we're going to get rid of all of them," said Dr. Gladstone, "and then what they've got is ours."

"Their heirs might have something to say about that," Ruby said.

"They will. They will. And now, dear, if twenty questions is done, I think we have to decide what to do with you."

The telephone rang. Dr. Gladstone answered it, then said "I'll be right there."

She replaced the phone and told Ruby: "Your friends have arrived. This Remo and Chiun. I have to go chase them first and then I'll be back to take care of you."

"I don't mind waiting," Ruby said.

"By the way, if you wish to yell, feel free. But this place is ten feet below the brownstone and is quite soundproof. No one will hear you yell, just as no one will hear you scream."

The doctor left and Ruby let out a hiss of air. That was one mean woman. With no time to waste, she began rocking her body back and forth on the hospi-

150

tal cot. She hoped that the wheels had not been locked in place.

They hadn't and a sudden jerk of her body was rewarded by the cot rolling two inches closer to the counter on which she saw the scalpel.

Two inches down. Ten feet to go. Ruby kept rocking.

Elena Gladstone smiled automatically as she walked into her book-lined main office in the front of the brownstone and saw Remo and Chiun sitting before her desk.

"How do you do?" she said. "I'm Dr. Gladstone. I understand you've been sent by Mr. Elmer Lippincott, Senior."

"That's right," Remo said. "My name is Williams. This is Chiun."

"You can call me Master," Chiun said.

"I'm pleased to meet you both," she said. She brushed past Remo as she walked behind her desk. She gave off a heavy femine scent, a scent her body deserved even if the stark white laboratory clothing she was wearing did not. He knew that scent from somewhere.

"What can I do for you?" she asked as she sat down.

"First, it was Lem Lippincott and then Randall," Remo said. "We wondered if you have any explanation for why they did what they did. Mr. Lippincott told us you're the family doctor."

"That's right," Elena said, but shook her head. "I don't know what happened to them. They were both in good health, or as good as sedentary men can be. They had no serious emotional problems that I know of. They weren't on drugs or any medication. I don't know what happened to them."

"Randall Lippincott was afraid of clothing," Remo said. "He couldn't stand having anything on his body."

"And I just don't understand that," Elena said. "I've never, in all these years, heard of such an irrational fear."

"You think you could have helped him?" Remo asked.

"I don't know. Perhaps. I would have tried. But I wasn't called when he became ill."

"What kind of work do you do here?" Remo asked.

"This is a life preservation facility. We try to find illnesses before they flare up. We do physical examinations whose goal is to prevent serious illness. If we find someone is losing the tone in his back muscles, for instance, and we have sophisticated ways of measuring that, we prescribe for them a series of exercise that will prevent the trouble before it begins."

"A big place just to look for bad backs," Remo said.

Elena Gladstone smiled at him. Her broad smile usually brought a response from men, an eagerness to please her. From this Remo Williams, it brought nothing but a deepening of his eyes, already dark pools sunk deep into his skull. He looked vaguely Oriental himself, she thought, and wondered if he were somehow related to the old Oriental who sat silently at her desk, examining the sharpened pencils in her pencil holder.

"It's not just bad backs," she said. "We work the entire range of potential health problems. Hearts,

152

blood pressure, chemical deficiencies in the body, arterial problems. Everything."

"And that's all you do?" Remo was obviously unimpressed, she thought.

"And we do some basic research on lab animals. That's more a hobby of mine than one of our main functions," she said. "Mr. Lippincott has been very generous in supporting our work."

Chiun had touched the tips of two pencils together, sharpened tip to sharpened tip. He was holding them together with just his index fingers on the rubber erasers. The two pencils were spread out in front of him, like one long pencil, with two points in the center and an eraser on each end. He seemed intent on the pencils. Remo looked at him and seemed annoyed.

Dr. Gladstone was interested. She had never seen that done before.

"With two of the Lippincott sons dead," Remo said, and she snapped back to attention toward him, "we have to worry about the third son."

"Douglas," she said.

Remo nodded. "Right. Douglas. Does he have any medical problems we should know about?"

"None. He's the youngest son. He exercises regularly and he's in good shape. I'd be very surprised if Douglas should turn up sick somehow."

Chiun was moving his hands in front of him, still holding the pencils, point to point. His hands made large circles in front of him and he was making small sounds under his breath, as if imitating an airplane engine.

"I see," said Remo. He was running out of subtle

questions. "We're looking for a black woman. Have you see her?"

"A black woman? Here? No. Was she supposed to be here?" Elena Gladstone felt the hazel eyes of the old Korean burning into her face.

"Not really," Remo said. "She's kind of an associate of ours and she said she might be here to meet us."

"Sorry. I haven't seen her yet. Can I give her a message if she comes?"

"No, that's all right," Remo said. He rose. "Chiun," he said.

Chiun turned his right hand palm up and slowly moved his left hand around so that the two palms faced each other, the distance of two pencils apart. As Dr. Gladstone watched, he removed his left hand and the two pencils touching only at their points remained balanced in the air above Chiun's right hand. Then he flipped the index finger on which they rested and the two pencils popped up into the air. Each turned one slow revolution and landed in the small opening of her pencilholder cup.

She clapped her hands in appreciative glee.

"Stop fooling around, Chiun," Remo snarled. "We've got work to do."

Chiun rose slowly to his feet.

"On your way out, I'll show you the rest of our operation," Dr. Gladstone said, also rising. She led them out into the reception room. "My living quarters are upstairs," she said. She turned down the hallway toward the lab. "On the sides here are our examination rooms. Here we do physicals and EKGs and monitor heart rates, stress tests, blood tests and such."

The doors to all the small offices were open and Ruby was not in any of them, Remo could see.

Remo again smelled the heady flowery scent of Elena Gladstone's perfume as she pushed through a door into a large, light laboratory, lined on both sides with cages of mice and rats and monkeys. The din was earsplitting.

"These are our laboratory animals," she said.

"What do you use them for?"

"We're trying to develop a new anti-stress drug," she said. "And of course you have to make animal tests. We're years away, I'm afraid."

Remo followed her along the line of cages. Chiun was walking behind him and he could hear Chiun thumping his feet. Remo wondered why.

"And that's it," Dr. Gladstone said. "The whole place."

"Thanks for your time, doctor," Remo said. He looked around the laboratory. His eyes rested on Chiun who had a faint smile on his face.

"What's down there?" Remo said, pointing down a short corridor.

"That's my lab office," Dr. Gladstone said. "Where I keep records of our experiments here. The office up front is for when I play administrator. This one is for when I'm playing researcher."

She smiled broadly at Remo who returned the smile.

"Sometime we'll have to get together to play doctor," he said.

"Yes," Elena Gladstone said, looking directly into his eyes. "Yes." Her body tingled.

She took Remo by the arm and led him back toward the front of the building. Chiun followed, stomping. Remo was ready to tell him to knock it off. The receptionist smiled at the two men as Dr. Gladstone led them to the front door.

"I hope to see you again," she said as Remo and Chiun stepped outside.

"I hope so," said Remo.

"You shall," said Chiun.

Dr. Gladstone closed the door behind them and when she saw through the peephole that they had walked down the steps of the building, she quietly locked the door.

"Call everyone scheduled today, Hazel, and cancel their appointments. I'm going to be very busy."

"I understand."

Outside, Remo and Chiun made a pretense of walking away from the house, but stopped in front of the next building.

"What do you think, Little Father?" Remo asked.

"She is lying, of course."

"I know. I recognized that perfume of hers. It was the smell in Randall Lippincott's room at the hopsital. She was the doctor who drugged him."

Chiun nodded. "The lady has a little vein visible in her neck. When you asked her about the black woman, the vein began to throb almost twice as fast as before. She was lying."

"Then Ruby's in there," Remo said.

"Correct."

"Where, I wonder?"

"In the basement," Chiun said.

"That's why you were stomping?" Remo said.

"Yes. There is a large room below the laboratory. I imagine that we will find Ruby there," Chiun said.

"I think we better go back and collect Ruby," Remo said.

"She will like that," said Chiun.

Ruby Gonzalez had gotten her right hand around the scalpel when she heard footsteps coming down the stairs.

With the small amount of freedom allowed her feet and legs, she braced her feet against the counter and pushed as hard as she could. The hospital cot rolled back across the floor to a slow stop. She was three feet shy of where she had started and she hoped Dr. Gladstone wouldn't notice.

Carefully, being sure not to drop it, Ruby turned the scalpel around in her right hand, so that its blade pointed toward her shoulder and slowly she began to saw at the canvas band that pinned down her right arm.

Dr. Gladstone came back into the large bright room.

"Your two friends have just left," she said.

Ruby looked at her but said nothing.

"They said there was no message for you in case you should arrive after they left." She smiled.

"They turkeys," Ruby said.

"Probably true," Dr. Gladstone said. "And now we have to take care of you."

She walked to the counter. Ruby saw her take a disposable hypodermic from a cabinet and root around in the cabinet until she found a vial of clear liquid.

She had her back to Ruby and Ruby sawed furiously with the scalpel at the band on her right wrist. She could feel the canvas weakening, then she felt the warm ooze of liquid down her hand. She had cut her wrist with the scalpel. She kept sawing.

Dr. Gladstone spoke with her back to Ruby. "I'd really like for you to go out in style. I could have tried something new and unusual. Perhaps a pathological fear of automobiles. Then put you into the middle of Times Square."

"Ain't nothing wrong with being afraid of cars in this town," Ruby said.

Dr. Gladstone filled the hypodermic with the clear fluid, then replaced the vial in the cabinet.

"No, I guess that's true enough," she said. "But we won't have time for that. It'll have to be something simple and direct, like curare in the bloodstream."

Ruby gave one last furious jab at the canvas band and felt it separate. She began to raise her right hand to cut away the band on her left wrist, but Dr. Gladstone turned and Ruby dropped her right hand to her side.

Dr. Gladstone, holding the hypodermic in front of her eyes, examining it, walked back toward Ruby.

With her left hand, she felt for the vein on the inside of Ruby's left elbow. She found it and pressed down the surrounding skin with her fingertips to make the vein protrude. She lowered the syringe to it.

"I'm sorry, my dear," she said.

"You sure are," Ruby said. She swung her right hand up from her side, putting as much force into it as she could with her body anchored. The scalpel glinted as it flashed past her eyes and then it bit into the left side of Elena Gladstone's neck and Ruby snapped her wrist on the follow-through as if she were wristing a little pitch shot onto the green.

The hypodermic fell to the highly-waxed white tile floor. Dr. Gladstone's eyes opened wide as she realized what had happened. A gusher of blood pumped from the side of her slashed throat.

She tried to scream, but all she could produce was a bubbling high-pitched shriek as she fell.

Outside, moving down the steps they had found behind the filing cabinet in Elena Gladstone's office, Remo and Chiun heard the sound.

Remo said, "Hurry, Chiun." He ran down the steps.

Chiun slowed up and smiled. "It is too late, Remo. Ruby does not need us."

Remo didn't hear him. He pushed his way through the heavy metal fire door into the large bright room.

Elena Gladstone lay on the floor, her dead body still pumping blood onto the tiles.

Ruby was using the bloodied scalpel to saw away the band on her left wrist.

She looked up as Remo came through the door. He stood there speechless.

"Remind me never to count on you for anything," Ruby screeched. Remo smiled and took the earplugs from his pocket and put them in his ears.

"Oh, shut up," he said with a smile.

Chiun came up behind him. He saw Ruby strapped to the cot and whispered to Remo:

"If you wish, I will leave and you can take advantage of her while she is a prisoner. But remember, the baby is mine."

"If you think I'm going near a black chick with a knife, you're crazy."

"Will you two stop jawing, and get me out of here? I'm tired of sawing," Ruby hollered.

CHAPTER FOURTEEN

Dr. Jesse Beers took the telephone call from Hazel, the young receptionist at the Lifeline Laboratory, in his room, two doors away from the master bedroom of Elmer Lippincott Sr. and his young wife, Gloria.

His face turned white as he listened. Then he said, "All right, Hazel. Just close up the lab. Lock everything up. Leave everything where it is." He paused. "Yes, her too. Just you lock up and go home and I'll come up later and take care of everything. No, no, don't call the police. I'll explain it all to you when I come to your house." He forced a smile. "I haven't been to your house for a while, sweetmeat, and I'm about ready."

He waited for the expected words of invitation and when they had come, he said: "Think of me. I'll be with you soon."

He hung up the telephone and walked down to the master bedroom.

Gloria Lippincott was alone in the room. Her belly swelling gently, she sat in front of the makeup dresser, applying mascara to her eyes.

"Elena's dead," Beers said as he closed the door behind him.

161

Gloria slowly put down the mascara tube and turned toward him.

"What happened?"

"I don't know. Our receptionist found her with her throat cut. She said she saw those two men your husband was with. The old Chink and the skinny dude."

"Goddamit, I guessed they were trouble when Elmer told me about them," Gloria said. "What about the receptionist? Will she talk?"

"No," Beers said. "I told her to lock up and go home and wait for me. She's got the hots for me. She'll wait."

"Doesn't everybody?" asked Gloria.

Jesse Beers grinned. "Present company included."

"Don't flatter yourself," Gloria said. "You're a tool with a tool and don't forget it."

"I know it," Beers said. He sounded deflated.

"And we're both in this for one thing only. The money. Certainly not because I like ruining my figure and walking around carrying this baby of yours in my belly."

"Who knows?" he said. "You might like it."

Gloria did not answer. She was drumming her fingers on the dressing table.

"All right," she finally said. "We've got to get rid of Douglas. Then you can split."

"What about the old man?" asked Beers.

"He can wait. Maybe later when all this blows over. Hell, he's eighty years old. He might just conk any minute without any help from us."

"I don't like it," Beers said. "Maybe we ought to just call everything off."

"Lover getting cold feet?" Gloria taunted. "Listen,

we've gone this far and we're not stopping now. I don't think anybody's going to connect Elena's death with Lem and Randall dying, but even suppose they did. You were here when both those twits died. You're just a doctor in residence making sure Elmer Lippincott's baby is born healthy and well."

Jesse Beers pursed his lips as he thought. Then he nodded.

"Where do I find Douglas?" he said.

"That's the beautiful part. He's here. The old man told him he wanted to see him."

"He's not going to tell what he did, is he?" asked Beers.

"No, you don't understand the Lippincotts, Jesse A little guilt goes a long way. So he was feeling guilty last night blaming himself for the two twerps' deaths. But it was all gone by morning. He just wants to talk to Douglas about handling more of the business, now that the brothers are dead."

"All right. How should I do it?"

She mulled a moment, sucking on the tip of her right index finger.

"I'll get Elmer to come up here and when I do you slip downstairs and get rid of the twerp."

Beers nodded.

"Can you make it look like his heart?"

"Sure," Beers said. "I've got medicines that can make anything look like anything."

"Good. Now get out of here and let me finish my eyes. I'll call Elmer up here in ten minutes. Then you can get Douglas in the study. But let me finish my eyes first." She smiled at Beers. "I want Elmer to stay up here with me for a while."

"Who wouldn't stay at your invitation?" Beers asked.

"Flatterer. Even with this belly you gave me?"

"If it was twice as big."

"Get away now and let me do my thing. Ten minutes, I'll have him here."

Remo drove. Chiun sat in the back seat while Ruby explained to them what she had learned from Dr. Gladstone.

"She was the one that killed the two Lippincotts," she said. "And Zack Meadows before that."

"Who's Zack Meadows?" Remo asked.

"He the detective who wrote the letter to the President about the plot to kill the Lippincotts. She killed him and somebody who tipped Meadows on what she was doing. Then she killed the two brothers."

"And she's dead now," Remo said, "so why are we racing up to the Lippincott estate?"

"Because of something she said," Ruby said.

"What'd she say?" asked Remo.

"Did she tell you what I did with the pencils?" Chiun asked.

"No," said Ruby.

"She seemed very impressed," Chiun said.

"What'd she say?" Remo repeated.

"I asked her why the Lippincotts," Ruby said. "And she said 'we're going to get rid of all of them'!"

"So what? She's dead," Remo said.

"She said 'we're.' Not her. She's got a partner in it."

"Or partners," Chiun said. " 'We're' could mean more than one extra person with her."

"That's right," Ruby said. "She say something else too."

"What's that?" Remo asked.

"She said the Lippincott money would be theirs. I said the heirs might have something to say about that. She said 'they will, they will.'"

"What does that mean?" Remo asked.

"Just that I think she's got a partner in the family."

"That old man," Remo said. "I didn't like that old man from the minute I met him."

"That's ageist," said Chiun. "That's the worst kind of ageist statement I've ever heard. Admit it, you didn't like him just because he was old."

"That's probably true," Remo said. "Old people are a pain in the ass. They kvetch and bicker and carp, day and night, night and day. If it's not elevators, it's notes under the door. There's always something for them to bitch about."

"Ageist. But what would you expect from somebody who's racist and sexist and imperialist?" Chiun said.

"Right on, Little Daddy," said Ruby.

Remo grunted and stepped harder on the gas pedal as the car thundered forward onto the New York Thruway, heading north toward the Lippincott estate.

Elmer Lippincott Sr. was feeling better. His young wife always knew the way to cheer him up. Last night, he had felt guilt-ridden at the death of two sons, but today, he was able to see it in perspective. First of all, they weren't his sons. He hadn't any sons. Dr. Gladstone at the Lifeline Laboratory had

165

proved that conclusively, not only with blood tests conducted without the Lippincott sons' knowledge, but also by proving indisputably to the senior Lippincott that he had been sterile all his life. He had been unable to father children. Those three—Lem and Randall and Douglas—nothing but the offspring of a cheating wife, now blessedly dead, thank you.

So Gloria had explained to him, there really wasn't much to feel guilty about. But they were dead, and he hadn't really wanted them dead.

Gloria had held him in her arms and explained that away too.

"They were unavoidable accidents," she said. "You didn't plan it that way and you can't blame yourself for their deaths. Just accidents."

And he had thought about it and felt better and soon he would have a son of his own thanks to Dr. Gladstone's fertility drugs, which made him a man again and helped him to fill Gloria with his own son.

And what of Douglas, the surviving Lippincott son? Well, it wasn't his fault that his mother had been a cheat, cuckolding her husband. Elmer Lippincott would treat him just like a son for the rest of his life.

He had decided that and he was in the middle of a good early-morning meeting with his son when the telephone rang.

"Yes, dear," he said. "Of course. I'll be right up. Shall I bring Douglas? Oh, I see." He hung up the phone and told his son: "Doug, wait for me, will you? Gloria has to talk to me about something. I'll be right down."

"Sure thing, Pop," said Douglas Lippincott. He was the youngest of the three sons and the most like

166

the senior Lippincott. He moved with a muscular kind of energy that years of sitting in boardrooms and bankers' offices hadn't been able to destroy. Elmer Lippincott had often thought that of the three boys, Douglas was the only one he'd like to have on his side in a saloon fight.

As the old man left the office on the first floor of the mansion, Douglas Lippincott smiled. Young Gloria certainly had the old man's nose. When she said bark, he barked, and when she said come, he came. He wondered how she was taking the double tragedies that had hit the Lippincott family, but he suspected she'd be able to bear up under the anguish. He had watched her house-counting eyes too many times to be fooled into thinking that she loved the old man for the old man's sake. It was the Lippincott billions that she really loved.

Douglas walked to the corner of the room where there was a desk ashtray with a telescoping collapsible golf putter built into the side of it. He had given it to his father years before to try to convince him to relax. But the old man would have none of it. He had never used the putter.

There was a round rubber eraser on the old man's desk and Douglas put a paper cup on the floor, opened the putter to its full length, then from six feet away tried to roll the eraser into the cup. It bounced along the carpet unevenly and at the last moment, swung away and missed the cup completely.

Douglas fished it back with the putter and was lining up the shot again when the door opened behind him. He turned around expecting to see his father.

Instead, he saw Dr. Jesse Beers, who was walking like Napoleon, both hands clasped behind him.

Douglas Lippincott didn't like Jesse Beers either. The man always seemed to be scheming something. He turned back to his putt.

"Hello, Doctor," he said

"Good morning, Mister Lippincott."

As he lined up the putt, Douglas realized it was strange for Beers to walk into Elmer Lippincott's office without knocking. And now that he was here, what did he want? He turned to ask and as he turned he saw Beers moving toward him. The man had a hypodermic in his hand.

Douglas tried to swing at Beers with the putter but he was too close and Beers was able to grab it and yanked it from Douglas's hands.

"What the hell do you think you're doing?" he asked.

"Tidying up loose ends," Beers said. "Now take your medicine like a good little boy."

He advanced toward Douglas with the syringe in one hand, the golf club in the other.

"I promise it won't hurt," he said.

"Up yours," said Douglas. He reached his hand up to the bookcase behind him, grabbed an armful of books and tossed them at Beers. One hit the syringe and knocked it to the gold colored carpeting on the floor.

Beers dove for the needle and Lippincott came after him to grapple for it. But Beers grabbed the handle of the putter and swung it at Lippincott. It caught him on the side of the jaw, laying open his skin and knocking him to the floor.

He lay there groggily while Beers picked up the syringe and came toward him again.

He reached down for Lippincott's arm. Then he heard a voice.

"You lose."

Lippincott looked up dazedly. In the doorway stood a lean, dark-haired man. Behind him was a black woman and an old Oriental in a yellow robe.

"Who the hell are you?" snarled Beers. "Get out of here."

"Game's over," Remo said.

Beers growled and waving the hypodermic over his head like a miniature spear, raced at Remo, his face contorted with rage and furey.

Lippincott shook his head to clear it. He wanted to shout to the thin man in the doorway that Beers was dangerous. He blinked. When he opened his eyes again, the thin man was inside the room, behind Beers. Beers was upon the old Oriental. The old man, without even seeming to move, spun Beers about until he was facing back into the room, then propelled him toward the thin man.

As Beers came within reach, Remo moved in, removed the syringe from his hand, and tapped him in the thick part of his left leg, halfway between knee and hip. The doctor's leg gave way and Beers fell to the carpeted floor.

Remo tossed the syringe on the desk, and turned his back on Beers. He asked Lippincott:

"You Douglas?"

Lippincott nodded.

"You okay?"

"I'll live," Douglas said.

"You'll be the first one this week," Remo said. He turned back to Beers. As he did, Ruby moved in and stood by the desk.

"All right, sweetheart," Remo said. "Hard or easy?"

"I want a lawyer," Beers said. "I'll have your ass."

"Hard," Remo said. "Have it your way." Remo's hand spun out and he grabbed the lobe of Beers's left ear. He twisted it. It felt to Beers as if it were coming off.

"Easy," he yelled. "Easy, easy."

Remo relaxed his grip and Jesse Beers talked. He told everything. The plot; how it worked; who was behind it; how the conspirators had conned Elmer Lippincott Sr. As he spoke, Douglas Lippincott raised himself to a sitting position. The blood flow down his cheek had slowed to a trickle and his eyes lit up with anger. He got slowly to his feet, and walked alongside Remo, glaring down at Beers.

"Let that bastard go," he told Remo.

"What for?" Remo asked.

"I want him," Douglas Lippincott said.

"All yours," Remo said. He released Beers's ear and stepped back. Lippincott reached back his fist to punch the taller, heavier doctor. But at the last second, Beers scrambled to his feet and ran to the desk. He reached around Ruby for the syringe, but she held it in her hand behind her back. Beers lifted his hand to hit Ruby. She swung the syringe around, buried it deep into Beers's side and depressed the plunger.

"Ow," Beers yelled. Then he looked down at the syringe in her hand. He looked up at her face, questioning, panic and fear in his eyes. He turned to look around the room. At Remo. At Chiun, who was examining the paintings on the walls, at Douglas Lip-

170

pincott. The faces he saw were hard and uncaring. He tried to speak but no words would come, and he felt his heart begin to pound, and his limbs grow leaden, and his eyes start to close, and then it was hard to breathe, and his brain told him to cry out for help, but before he could, the messages stopped coming from the brain and Jesse Beers fell to the floor dead.

Lippincott looked down in shock. He looked up at Ruby who was nonchalantly examining the syringe. Chiun continued to examine the paintings, shaking his head and clucking. Remo spied the putter on the floor and said to Lippincott "This yours?"

"No. My father's," Lippincott said. "Hey, this man is dead. Don't any of you care?"

"No business of mine," Ruby said. Chiun asked Lippincott how much the oil painting on the wall was worth. Remo said, "You're trying to putt this eraser into that cup?"

Lippincott nodded.

"It won't roll true," Remo said.

"I found that out," Lippincott said.

"You have to chip it in," Remo said. He dropped the putter head sharply onto the back edge of the eraser. It popped the lump of rubber up into the air and it plopped heavily into the paper cup six feet away.

"See? Like that," Remo said. "Actually, I'm a pretty good putter."

Lippincott shook his head. "I don't know who you people are, but I guess I should thank you."

"About time too," Chiun said.

"Now I've got some business to transact," Douglas said.

"Mind if we come along?" Remo said. "Just to close the books?"

"Be my guest," Lippincott said.

"Good," said Ruby still holding the syringe. "I love family arguments. When they ain't my family.'

"If your family's like you," Remo said, stepping over Jesse Beers's corpse, "don't argue with them. They're all prone to violence."

CHAPTER FIFTEEN

"Are you feeling better now, dear?" Elmer Lippincott Sr. paced nervously alongside the bed, where his wife lay under a thin satin sheet.

"Yes, darling," Gloria said. "I'm sorry. Just for a moment there, I was depressed. I thought . . . well, I thought, what if something goes wrong with the baby?"

"Nothing will go wrong," Lippincott said. "That's why we've got Beers here. Where is he anyway?"

"No, Elmer, it's all right. I called him and he examined me and said there was nothing wrong. But, well, he's not you, sweetheart. I needed you. I'm all right now. You can go back to your meeting."

"If you're sure," Lippincott said.

"I'm sure. Go. I'm going to rest and get my strength so I can give you the nicest son."

Lippincott nodded. A voice behind him said, "A son, but why don't you tell him whose it is?"

Elmer Lippincott wheeled, his face red with anger. Douglas stood in the doorway. Behind him Lippincott saw the man Remo and the old Oriental and a young black woman.

"What the hell do you mean by that, Douglas?"

Douglas Lippincott stepped into the room.

"You fool," he snapped. "They say there's no fool like an old fool and I guess you prove that. That's not your son she's carrying, you goddam simp."

"I'll remind you where you are and you're aren't welcome here any longer," Lippincott said. "It'd be better if you left."

"I'll leave when I'm goddam good and ready," Douglas said. "But first I'm going to tell you what happened and how you managed to be the partner in the murder of two of your sons."

"They weren't my sons, if you want to know. Neither are you. Three bastards," Lippincott said.

"You senile, doddering idiot. That was a line they fed you. Dr. Gladstone and Beers, they were working together. First they conned you with that story that you had been sterile all your life and we weren't your sons. Then they steamed you up to punish us and they killed Lem and Randall."

The old man looked confused. He looked past his son at Chiun who nodded. He looked at Remo who said, "What do you want from me? Listen to your kid for a change."

"Why?" asked Lippincott.

"You clown," Douglas said. "So they shoot you up with monkey hormones so you feel like a young goat again and you go sailing off with that cheap piece of trim." He pointed at Gloria who shouted "No, no, no," and sank down in the bed.

"But the joke is on you, dear father," Douglas said. " 'Cause you *are* sterile now and have been for years, and that baby that sweetie pie there is carrying isn't yours. In three months, you're going to be the proud doting parent of the son of Dr. Jesse Beers."

Lippincott wheeled. "Gloria. Tell him he's lying."

"Yeah, Gloria. tell me I'm lying," Douglas said.

"I hate you," Gloria hissed at Douglas. The breath came out of her like a deflating innertube. "I hate you."

Lippincott saw that she refused to deny the charge. He sank down onto the bed.

"But why?" he sobbed. "Why?"

"For your money," Douglas said. "Why else? She was going to give you a little bastard kid and kill us off and then when the kid was born, kill you off and she and Dr. Gladstone and Dr. Beers and all these nice beautiful people were going to live happily ever after. Isn't that right, Gloria?"

Remo turned to Ruby. "Kid's all right," he said.

"Not bad," Ruby agreed. "A little talky maybe, but basically pretty good."

"If you two are talking about an heir for me," Chiun said, "I wish you wouldn't whisper. I want to know about it."

"You'll be the first to know," Ruby said. "When and if."

Elmer Lippincott buried his face in his hands and wept.

Douglas spat the words at him. "And now, you old son of a bitch, I'm leaving this house. I'm going back to my businesses and I'm going to run you out of them. You may control more stock that I do, Daddy dear, but I know what makes them work and I'm going to shove them down your throat. By the time your sweet little son is born. . . ." He left the sentence unfinished.

"You'd destroy our empire?" his father said.

"No. I'm going to make it bigger and better than ever. But I'm going to do it without you. And when your concubine foals and then you go on to the great board meeting in the sky, she'll just have to get along on a piece of what she expected. And who knows? Maybe you'll live to be a hundred. You can watch your bastard grow up and watch Gloria turn to fat and wrinkles and worry every day that she's putting rat poison in your pablum. Good luck, Daddy."

Douglas walked back to the door. "Thanks," he said to Remo.

"You're welcome," Remo said.

"Don't thank me," Chiun said. "I did everything and you thank him. Ageist."

"Let's go," Remo said, after Douglas left.

"Just a minute," Ruby said.

"What?" asked Remo.

"This is how it ends? You let it end like this? He kills his two sons, four, five other people are dead, and you just walk off into the sunset?"

Remo said, "It's not our business to hand out punishment to him. It's our job to see that no more Lippincotts get killed and that the Lippincott businesses don't go under. We've done it, so we go home."

Chiun nodded toward Elmer Lippincott, who was still weeping.

"He has suffered much already," Chiun said. "Whatever days are left to him will be lived with the knowledge that he killed his own sons." He glanced toward Remo. "And without extenuating circumstances."

Ruby shook her head.

"No," she said. "No way."

"What do you mean," Remo asked.

"Maybe you let it go like that but I don't," Ruby said. "Life ain't that cheap." She turned to a table

176

behind them and fumbled with a glass. Remo looked at Chiun and shrugged.

Her right hand behind her, Ruby walked to the bed where Lippincott still sat.

He paid no attention as she unbuttoned the cuff of his shirt and slowly pulled up his left sleeve. When she had exposed his bicep, she took a hypodermic syringe from behind her, jammed it into his muscle and squeezed.

Lippincott jumped at the shock. He slapped at his arm but Ruby had already removed the syringe.

"What?" he sputtered.

Ruby stared down at him, her eyes flashing.

"You wanna know what?" she said. "Just a little magic medicine from Dr. Gladstone's house of horrors."

"But what?"

"I don't know. I didn't bother to ask," Ruby said. "But some of her experiment stuff. Maybe it makes you afraid of the dark and you'll die some night when the bulb in your nightlight burns out. Maybe it makes you afraid of high places and someday you'll be up on one of your skyscrapers and you'll get afraid and figure out the best way down is to jump. I don't know, sucker. I hope it makes you afraid of money 'cause you'd deserve that one." She looked across at Gloria. "I'm just sorry, lady, that I didn't save enough for you, too. But I wouldn't wanna hurt the doctor's baby."

She walked back to Remo and Chiun.

"*Now* we're done," she said. "Let's go."

In the hallway, she dropped the hypodermic into her purse. They walked in silence down to their car, parked in front of the mansion.

As they were getting into the car, Remo asked her:

"What was in the syringe?"

"Water," Ruby said. "But Lippincott there doesn't ever have to know that."

"Do you think there is any kind of drug that would make him want to buy a painting of me?" Chiun asked.

"There's no drug that strong," Remo said.

An insider's view of the *Death Merchant*— A master of disguise, deception, and destruction . . . and his job is death.

DEATH MERCHANT
by Joseph Rosenberger

One of Pinnacle's best-selling action series is the Death Merchant, *which tells the story of an unusual man who is a master of disguise and an expert in exotic and unusual firearms: Richard Camellion. Dedicated to eliminating injustice from the world, whether on a personal, national, or international level, possessed of a coldly logical mind, totally fearless, he has become over the years an unofficial, unrecognized, but absolutely essential arm of the CIA. He takes on the dirty jobs, the impossible missions, the operations that cannot be handled by the legal or extralegal forces of this or other sympathetic countries. He is a man without a face, without a single identifying characteristic. He is known as the master of the three Ds—Death, Destruction, and Disguise. He is, in fact and in theory, the Death Merchant.*

The conception of the "Death Merchant" did not involve any instant parthenogenesis, but a parentage whose partnership is more ancient than recorded history. The father of Richard Camellion was *Logic*. The mother, *Realism*.

Logic involved the realization that people who read fiction want to be entertained and that real-life truth is often stranger and more fantastic than the most imaginative kind of fiction. Realism embraced the truth that any human being, having both emotional and physical weaknesses, is prone to mistakes and can accomplish only so much in any given situation.

We are born into a world in which we find ourselves surrounded by physical objects. There seems to be still another—a subjective—world within us, capable of receiving and retaining impressions from the outside world. Each one is a world of its own, with a relation to space different from that of the other. Collectively, these impressions and how they are perceived on the *individual* level make each human being a distinct person, an entity with his own views and opinions, his own likes and dislikes, his own personal strengths and weaknesses.

As applied to the real world, this means that the average human is actually a complex personality, a bundle of traits that very often are in conflict with each other, traits that are both good and bad. In fiction this means that the writer must show his chief character to be "human," i.e., to give the hero a multiplicity of traits, some good, some bad.

At the same time, Logic demands that in action-adventure the hero cannot be a literal superman and achieve the impossible. Our hero cannot jump into a crowd of fifty villains and flatten them with his bare hands—even if he is the best karate expert in the world! Sheer weight of numbers would bring him to his knees.

Accordingly, the marriage between Logic and Realism had to be, out of necessity, a practical union, one that would have to live in two worlds: the world of actuality and the world of fiction. This partnership would have to take the best from these two worlds to conceive a lead character who, while incredible in his deeds, could have a counterpart in the very real world of the living.

Conception was achieved. The Death Merchant was

born in February of 1971, in the first book of the series, *Death Merchant*.

This genesis was not without the elements that would shape the future accomplishments of Richard J. Camellion. Just as a real human being is the product of his gene-ancestry and, to a certain extent, of his environment during his formative years, so the fictional Richard Camellion also has a history, although one will have to read the entire series to glean his background and training.

There are other continuities and constants within the general structure of the series. For example, it might seem that the Death Merchant tackles the absurd and the inconceivable. He doesn't. He succeeds in his missions because of his training and experience, with emphasis on the former—training in the arts and sciences, particularly in the various disciplines that deal not only with the physical violence and self-defense, but with the various tricks of how to stay alive—self-preservation!

There are many other cornerstones that form the foundation of the general story line:

•Richard Camellion abhors boredom, loves danger and adventure, and feels that he may as well derive a good income from these qualities. The fact that he often has to take a human life does not make him brutal and cruel.

•Richard Camellion works for money; he's a modern mercenary. Nevertheless, he is a man with moral convictions and deeply rooted loyalties. He will not take on any job if its success might harm the United States.

•The Death Merchant usually works for the CIA or some other U.S. government agency. The reason is very simple. Richard Camellion handles only the most dangerous projects and/or the biggest threats. In today's world the biggest battles involve the silent but very real war being waged beween the various intelligence communities of the world. This war is basically between freedom and tyranny, between Democracy and Communism.

(The Death Merchant has worked for non-government agencies, but he has seldom worked for individuals because few can pay his opening fee: $100,000. Usually, those individuals who could and would pay his fee, such as members of organized crime, couldn't buy his special talents for ten times that, cash in advance.)

•The Death Merchant is a pragmatic realist. He is not a hypocrite and readily admits that he works mainly for money. In his words, "While money doesn't bring happiness, if you have a lot of the green stuff you can be unhappy in maximum comfort." Yet he has been known to give his entire fee—one hundred grand—to charity!

•Richard Camellion *did not* originate the title "Death Merchant." He hates the title, considering it both silly and incongruous. But he can't deny it. He *does* deal in death. The nickname came about because of his deadly proficiency with firearms and other devices of the quick-kill. (All men die, and Camellion knows that it is only a question of *when*. He has never feared death, "Which is maybe one reason why I have lived as long as I have.")

•The weapons and equipment used in the series do exist. (Not only does the author strive for realism and authenticity, but technical advice is constantly being furnished by Lee E. Jurras, the noted ballistician and author.)

Another support of the general plot is that Camellion is a master of disguise and makeup, and a superb actor as well.

It can be said that Richard Camellion, the Death

Merchant, is the heart of the series; but *action*—fast-paced, violent, often bloody—is the life's blood that keeps the heart pumping. This is not merely a conceptual device of the author; it is based on realistic considerations. The real world *is* violent. Evil *does* exist. The world of adventure and of espionage is especially violent.

The Death Merchant of 1971 is not necessarily the same Death Merchant of 1978. In organizing the series, we did use various concepts in constructing the background and the character of Richard Camellion.

Have any of these concepts changed?

The only way to answer the question is to say that while these concepts are still there and have not changed as such, many of them have not matured and are still in the limbo of "adolescence." For example:

We have not elaborated on several phases of his early background, or given any reasons why Camellion decided to follow a life of danger. He loves danger? An oversimplification. Who first called him the Death Merchant? What kind of training did he have? At times he will murmur, *"Dominus Lucis vobiscum."* What do the words "The Lord of Life be with you" mean to Camellion?

All the answers, and more, will be found in future books in the series.

Camellion's role is obvious. He's the "good guy" fighting on the side of justice. He's a man of action who is very sure of himself in anything he undertakes; a ruthless, cold-blooded cynic who doesn't care if he lives or dies; an expert killing machine whose mind runs in only one groove: getting the job done. One thing is certain: he is not a Knight on a White Horse! He has all the flaws and faults that any human being can have.

Camellion is a firm believer in law, order, and justice, but he doesn't think twice about bending any law and, if necessary, breaking it. He's an individualist, honest in his beliefs, a nonconformist.

He also seems to be a health nut. He doesn't smoke, indulges very lightly in alcohol, is forever munching on "natural" snacks (raisins, nuts, etc.), and uses Yoga methods of breathing and exercise.

Richard Camellion is not the average champion/hero. He never makes a move unless the odds are on his side. He may *seem* reckless, but he isn't.

Richard Camellion wouldn't turn down a relationship with a woman, but he doesn't go out of his way to find one. The great love of his life is weapons, particularly his precious Auto Mags.

As a whole, readers' reactions are very favorable to the series. It is they who keep Richard Camellion alive and healthy.

The real father and mother of Richard Camellion is Joseph Rosenberger. A professional writer since the age of 21, when he sold an article, he worked at various jobs before turning to fulltime writing in 1961. Rosenberger is the author of almost 2,000 published short stories and articles and 150 books, both fiction and nonfiction, writing in his own name and several pseudonyms. He originated the first kung fu fiction books, under the name of "Lee Chang." Among other things, he has been a circus pitchman, an instructor in "Korean karate," a private detective, and a free-lance journalist.

Unlike the Death Merchant, the author is not interested in firearms, and does not like to travel. He is the father of a 23-year-old daughter, lives and writes in Buffalo Grove, Illinois, and is currently hard at work on the latest adventure of Richard Camellion, the Death Merchant.

CELEBRATING 10 YEARS IN PRINT
AND OVER 20 MILLION COPIES SOLD!

☐ 41-216-9 Created, The Destroyer #1	$1.95	☐ 41-238-X Child's Play #23	$1.95
☐ 41-217-7 Death Check #2	$1.95	☐ 41-239-8 King's Curse #24	$1.95
☐ 40-879-X Chinese Puzzle #3	$1.75	☐ 40-901-X Sweet Dreams #25	$1.75
☐ 40-880-3 Mafia Fix #4	$1.75	☐ 40-902-3 In Enemy Hands #26	$1.75
☐ 40-881-1 Dr. Quake #5	$1.75	☐ 41-242-8 Last Temple #27	$1.95
☐ 40-882-X Death Therapy #6	$1.75	☐ 41-243-6 Ship of Death #28	$1.95
☐ 41-222-3 Union Bust #7	$1.95	☐ 40-905-2 Final Death #29	$1.75
☐ 40-884-6 Summit Chase #8	$1.75	☐ 40-110-8 Mugger Blood #30	$1.50
☐ 41-224-X Murder's Shield #9	$1.95	☐ 40-907-9 Head Men #31	$1.75
☐ 40-284-8 Terror Squad #10	$1.50	☐ 40-908-7 Killer Chromosomes #32	$1.75
☐ 41-226-6 Kill Or Cure #11	$1.95	☐ 40-909-5 Voodoo Die #33	$1.75
☐ 40-888-9 Slave Safari #12	$1.75	☐ 40-156-6 Chained Reaction #34	$1.50
☐ 41-228-2 Acid Rock #13	$1.95	☐ 41-250-9 Last Call #35	$1.95
☐ 40-890-0 Judgment Day #14	$1.75	☐ 40-912-5 Power Play #36	$1.75
☐ 40-289-9 Murder Ward #15	$1.50	☐ 41-252-5 Bottom Line #37	$1.95
☐ 40-290-2 Oil Slick #16	$1.50	☐ 40-160-4 Bay City Blast #38	$1.50
☐ 41-232-0 Last War Dance #17	$1.95	☐ 41-254-1 Missing Link #39	$1.95
☐ 40-894-3 Funny Money #18	$1.75	☐ 40-714-9 Dangerous Games #40	$1.75
☐ 40-895-1 Holy Terror #19	$1.75	☐ 40-715-7 Firing Line #41	$1.75
☐ 41-235-5 Assassins Play-Off #20	$1.95	☐ 40-716-5 Timber Line #42	$1.95
☐ 41-236-3 Deadly Seeds #21	$1.95	☐ 40-717-3 Midnight Man #43	$1.95
☐ 40-898-6 Brain Drain #22	$1.75		

Canadian orders must be paid with U.S. Bank check or U.S. Postal money order only.

Buy them at your local bookstore or use this handy coupon.

Clip and mail this page with your order

(◎) **PINNACLE BOOKS, INC.—Reader Service Dept.**
1430 Broadway, New York, NY 10018

Please send me the book(s) I have checked above. I am enclosing $ _____ (please add
75¢ to cover postage and handling). Send check or money order only—no cash or C.O.D.'s.

Mr./Mrs./Miss _____

Address _____

City _____ State/Zip _____

Please allow six weeks for delivery. Prices subject to change without notice.

DEATH MERCHANT

by Joseph Rosenberger

More bestselling action/adventure
from Pinnacle, America's #1 series publisher.
Over 5 million copies
of Death Merchant in print!

☐ 41-345-9 Death Merchant #1	$1.95	☐ 40-078-0 Budapest Action #23 $1.25
☐ 40-417-4 Operation Overkill #2	$1.50	☐ 40-352-6 Kronos Plot #24 $1.50
☐ 40-458-1 Psychotron Plot #3	$1.50	☐ 40-117-5 Enigma Project #25 $1.25
☐ 40-418-2 Chinese Conspiracy #4	$1.50	☐ 40-118-3 Mexican Hit #26 $1.50
☐ 40-419-0 Satan Strike #5	$1.50	☐ 40-119-1 Surinam Affair #27 $1.50
☐ 40-459-X Albanian Connection #6	$1.50	☐ 40-833-1 Nipponese Nightmare #28 $1.75
☐ 40-420-4 Castro File #7	$1.50	☐ 40-272-4 Fatal Formula #29 $1.50
☐ 40-421-2 Billionaire Mission #8	$1.50	☐ 40-385-2 Shambhala Strike #30 $1.50
☐ 22-594-6 Laser War #9	$1.25	☐ 40-392-5 Operation Thunderbolt #31 $1.50
☐ 40-815-3 Mainline Plot #10	$1.75	☐ 40-475-1 Deadly Manhunt #32 $1.50
☐ 40-816-1 Manhattan Wipeout #11	$1.75	☐ 40-476-X Alaska Conspiracy #33 $1.50
☐ 40-817-X KGB Frame #12	$1.75	☐ 41-378-5 Operation Mind-Murder #34 $1.95
☐ 40-497-2 Mato Grosso Horror #13	$1.50	☐ 40-478-6 Massacre in Rome #35 $1.50
☐ 40-819-6 Vengeance: Golden Hawk #14	$1.75	☐ 41-380-7 Cosmic Reality Kill #36 $1.95
☐ 22-823-6 Iron Swastika Plot #15	$1.25	☐ 40-701-7 Bermuda Triangle Action #37 $1.75
☐ 22-911-9 Nightmare in Algeria #18	$1.25	☐ 41-382-3 The Burning Blue Death #38 $1.95
☐ 40-460-3 Armageddon, USA! #19	$1.50	☐ 41-383-1 The Fourth Reich #39 $1.95
☐ 40-256-2 Hell in Hindu Land #20	$1.50	☐ 41-018-2 Blueprint Invisibility #40 $1.75
☐ 40-826-9 Pole Star Secret #21	$1.75	☐ 41-019-0 The Shamrock Smash #41 $1.75
☐ 40-827-7 Kondrashev Chase #22	$1.75	☐ 41-020-4 High Command Murder #42 $1.95

Canadian orders must be paid with U.S. Bank check or U.S. Postal money order only.

Buy them at your local bookstore or use this handy coupon.

Clip and mail this page with your order

◎ **PINNACLE BOOKS, INC.—Reader Service Dept.**
271 Madison Ave., New York, NY 10016

Please send me the book(s) I have checked above. I am enclosing $_____ (please add 75¢ to cover postage and handling). Send check or money order only—no cash or C.O.D.'s.

Mr./Mrs./Miss _____

Address _____

City _____ State/Zip _____

Please allow six weeks for delivery. Prices subject to change without notice.

BLADE

by Jeffrey Lord

More bestselling heroic fantasy from Pinnacle, America's #1 series publisher.
Over 3.5 million copies of Blade in print!

☐ 40-432-8 The Bronze Axe #1	$1.50		☐ 40-793-9 Guardian Coral Throne #20	$1.75
☐ 40-433-6 Jewel of Tharn #3	$1.50		☐ 40-257-0 Champion of the Gods #21	$1.50
☐ 40-434-4 Slave of Sarma #4	$1.50		☐ 40-457-3 Forests of Gleor #22	$1.50
☐ 40-435-2 Liberator of Jedd #5	$1.50		☐ 40-263-5 Empire of Blood #23	$1.50
☐ 40-436-0 Monster of the Maze #6	$1.50		☐ 40-260-0 Dragons of Englor #24	$1.50
☐ 40-437-9 Pearl of Patmos #7	$1.50		☐ 40-444-1 Torian Pearls #25	$1.50
☐ 40-438-7 Undying World #8	$1.50		☐ 40-193-0 City of the Living Dead #26	$1.50
☐ 40-439-5 Kingdom of Royth #9	$1.50		☐ 40-205-8 Master of the Hashomi #27	$1.50
☐ 40-440-9 Ice Dragon #10	$1.50		☐ 40-206-6 Wizard of Rentoro #28	$1.50
☐ 40-441-7 King of Zunga #12	$1.75		☐ 40-207-4 Treasure of the Stars #29	$1.50
☐ 40-787-4 Temples of Ayocan #14	$1.75		☐ 40-208-2 Dimension of Horror #30	$1.50
☐ 40-442-5 Towers of Melnon #15	$1.50		☐ 40-648-7 Gladiators of Hapanu #31	$1.75
☐ 40-790-4 Mountains of Brega #17	$1.75		☐ 40-679-7 Pirates of Gohar #32	$1.50
☐ 22-855-4 Looters of Tharn #19	$1.25		☐ 40-852-8 Killer Plants of Binaark #33	$1.75

Canadian orders must be paid with U.S. Bank check or U.S. Postal money order only.

Buy them at your local bookstore or use this handy coupon.
Clip and mail this page with your order

PINNACLE BOOKS, INC.—Reader Service Dept.
271 Madison Ave., New York, NY 10016

Please send me the book(s) I have checked above. I am enclosing $_____ (please add 75¢ to cover postage and handling). Send check or money order only—no cash or C.O.D.'s.

Mr./Mrs./Miss _____

Address _____

City _____ State/Zip _____

Please allow six weeks for delivery. Prices subject to change without notice.

by Lionel Derrick

THE PENETRATOR

More bestselling action/adventure from Pinnacle, America's #1 series publisher!

☐ 40-101-9 Target Is H #1	$1.25
☐ 40-102-7 Blood on the Strip #2	$1.25
☐ 40-422-0 Capitol Hell #3	$1.50
☐ 40-423-9 Hijacking Manhattan #4	$1.50
☐ 40-424-7 Mardi Gras Massacre #5	$1.50
☐ 40-493-X Tokyo Purple #6	$1.50
☐ 40-494-8 Baja Bandidos #7	$1.50
☐ 40-495-6 Northwest Contract #8	$1.50
☐ 40-425-5 Dodge City Bombers #9	$1.50
☐ 40-957-5 Bloody Boston #12	$1.50
☐ 40-426-3 Dixie Death Squad #13	$1.50
☐ 40-427-1 Mankill Sport #14	$1.50
☐ 40-851-X Quebec Connection #15	$1.50
☐ 40-851-X Deepsea Shootout #16	$1.50
☐ 40-456-5 Demented Empire #17	$1.50
☐ 40-428-X Countdown to Terror #18	$1.50
☐ 40-258-9 Radiation Hit #20	$1.50
☐ 40-079-3 Supergun Mission #21	$1.25

☐ 40-067-5 High Disaster #22	$1.50
☐ 40-085-3 Divine Death #23	$1.50
☐ 40-177-9 Cryogenic Nightmare #24	$1.50
☐ 40-178-7 Floating Death #25	$1.50
☐ 40-179-5 Mexican Brown #26	$1.50
☐ 40-180-9 Animal Game #27	$1.50
☐ 40-268-6 Skyhigh Betrayers #28	$1.50
☐ 40-269-4 Aryan Onslaught #29	$1.50
☐ 40-270-8 Computer Kill #30	$1.50
☐ 40-363-1 Oklahoma Firefight #31	$1.50
☐ 40-514-6 Showbiz Wipeout #32	$1.50
☐ 40-513-8 Satellite Slaughter #33	$1.50
☐ 40-631-2 Death Ray Terror #34	$1.50
☐ 40-632-0 Black Massacre #35	$1.75
☐ 40-674-6 Candidate's Blood #37	$1.75
☐ 40-924-9 Cruise Into Chaos #39	$1.75
☐ 41-114-6 Assassination Factor #40	$1.75

Canadian orders must be paid with U.S. Bank check or U.S. Postal money order only.
Buy them at your local bookstore or use this handy coupon.
Clip and mail this page with your order

⊚ **PINNACLE BOOKS, INC.—Reader Service Dept.**
271 Madison Ave., New York, NY 10016

Please send me the book(s) I have checked above. I am enclosing $_____ (please add 75¢ to cover postage and handling). Send check or money order only—no cash or C.O.D.'s.

Mr./Mrs./Miss _____

Address _____

City _____ State/Zip _____

Please allow six weeks for delivery. Prices subject to change without notice.
